Hidden Love

SAPPHIC SECOND CHANCES

SAPPHIC SHELLEY

Copyright © 2024 by Sapphic Shelley

All rights reserved.

No part of this book may be reproduced in any form or by any electronic or mechanical means, including information storage and retrieval systems, without written permission from the author, except for the use of brief quotations in a book review.

Introduction

In a world where the past collides with the present, two women must navigate the tangled web of their shared history. Once enemies, now reluctant allies, Elena and Mira are brought together by fate and fueled by hidden emotions. As they confront their unresolved feelings, will they find the courage to transform their animosity into something deeper?

Hidden Love explores the complexities of love, forgiveness, and the possibility of second chances.

One

THE ICE CUBES clinked against the glass as Elena poured a precise stream of vodka over them, her fingers deftly twisting the bottle with practiced ease. She slid the drink across the polished bar to Jack, a regular who frequented The Ember Lounge on Thursday nights.

"Another perfect pour, Elena," Jack said, raising his glass in a toast. "You never disappoint."

Elena allowed a small smile to tug at her lips. "Years of practice," she replied smoothly. "And a healthy respect for the craft."

As she turned to replace the vodka bottle, her gaze drifted over the crowd mingling in the dimly lit lounge. The air was thick with the scents of perfume, cologne, and alcohol. Soft jazz music played in the background, the low notes of a saxophone weaving through the hum of conversation.

Suddenly, a flash of familiar auburn hair caught her eye, and her heart stuttered. It couldn't be... after all these years? Her hand faltered, splashing a few drops of vodka onto the bar, the sharp scent jolting her back to the present.

Quickly, she grabbed a cloth and wiped up the spill, mentally chastising herself for the lapse in focus. The past had a way of creeping up when she least expected it, threatening to shatter the walls she had built around her heart.

She risked another glance at the crowd, her pulse quickening as she searched for that telltale auburn hue. There—Mira. The name echoed in her mind like a half-forgotten melody, stirring memories of laughter under starlit skies, secrets whispered in the dark, and dreams woven together until betrayal severed their bond.

Elena tore her gaze away, forcing herself to concentrate on the task at hand. She had a business to run, customers to serve, a reputation to uphold. No room for ghosts from the past, no matter how compelling. She squared her shoulders, determination flooding her. She had risen from the ashes before, and she would do it again.

Elena finished preparing the cocktail, the clinking of ice a soothing counterpoint to her inner turmoil. She slid the drink across the bar, her lips curving into a practiced smile. "Enjoy," she murmured, her voice low and smooth.

As the customer turned away, Elena's gaze returned to Mira, who stood near the edge of the dance floor, her head tilted as she listened to a companion, a small smile playing on her lips. The sight was a punch to Elena's gut, a bitter reminder of all she had lost.

"Boss?" The tentative voice of her bartender, Javier, pulled her from her reverie.

"What is it, Javier?" she asked, her tone brisk.

"We're running low on lime wedges. Should I prep more?"

Elena nodded, grateful for the distraction. "Yes, and make sure we have enough glasses for the next rush. I don't want to be caught off guard."

Javier bobbed his head. "You got it, boss."

As he hurried away, Elena allowed herself a small smile. Javier was young but eager to learn, and she saw a bit of herself in his determination. Moments like these reminded her why she poured her heart into The Ember Lounge—to create a place where people could find a fresh start.

But even as she savored that small victory, she couldn't shake the awareness of Mira's presence, like a phantom limb that ached with every movement. She forced herself to focus on mixing drinks and chatting with customers while a part of her remained attuned to the woman who had once been her entire world.

As the night wore on, Elena found herself stealing glances at Mira, her curiosity warring with caution. What was she doing here? Had she come to gloat, or was there some hidden agenda?

The questions swirled in her mind, taunting her with possibilities she dared not contemplate. For now, all she could do was keep her guard up and emotions in check, lest she risk losing everything she had worked so hard to build. But even as she clung to her resolve, Elena couldn't help but wonder what the future might hold and whether the ghosts of her past would ever truly be laid to rest.

* * *

Elena slipped into her office, the muffled sounds of the lounge fading as she closed the door behind her. In the sanctuary of this space, she allowed herself a moment to breathe, to let the mask of composure slip just a fraction. She leaned against the door, eyes closed, and drew in a shaky breath, the weight of the evening's emotions pressing down upon her like a physical force.

Unbidden, a memory surged to the forefront of her mind, vivid and raw. She and Mira, years younger, laughing together in the golden light of a summer afternoon. They had been inseparable then, two halves of a single soul, bound by a friendship that seemed unbreakable. But even the strongest bonds could be shattered, and theirs had crumbled like sand beneath the weight of betrayal.

Elena's throat tightened as she recalled the moment everything had changed. The accusation in Mira's eyes, the disbelief and anger in her voice as she hurled words like weapons, each one finding its mark with unerring precision. "How could you?" she had demanded, tears streaming down her face. "I trusted you, Elena. I trusted you with everything, and you threw it all away."

The memory of that day still haunted Elena, the pain as fresh as if it had happened yesterday. She had tried to explain, to make Mira understand, but the damage had been done. The trust between them, once so strong, had shattered like glass, leaving only jagged edges and bleeding wounds.

In the years since, Elena had built a new life for herself, one shaped by the lessons of that bitter betrayal. She had learned to guard her heart, to keep her distance from those who might seek to hurt her. The Ember Lounge had become her refuge, a place where she could lose herself in the rhythm of work and the thrum of music, where she could forget, if only for a little while, the ache that still lingered in her chest.

But now, with Mira's sudden reappearance, all the old wounds had been ripped open anew. Elena could feel the familiar pain welling up inside her, the hurt and anger and longing that she had tried so hard to bury. She clenched her fists, nails biting into her palms, and forced herself to take a deep, steadying breath.

She couldn't let herself be thrown off balance, not now. She had worked too hard, come too far, to let the ghosts of her past drag her back down. Whatever Mira's reason for being here, Elena would face it with the same strength and determination that had carried her through all the trials of the last few years.

With a final, calming exhalation, Elena straightened her spine and squared her shoulders. She smoothed the wrinkles from her blouse, tucked a stray lock of hair behind her ear, and fixed her features into a mask of cool professionalism. Then, with a final glance around the sanctuary of her office, she turned and stepped back out into the lounge, ready to face whatever the night might bring.

* * *

Elena slipped into her office, the muffled sounds of the lounge fading as she closed the door behind her. In this sanctuary, she allowed herself a moment to breathe, letting the mask of composure slip just a fraction. Leaning against the door with her eyes closed, she drew in a shaky breath, the weight of the evening pressing down on her like a physical force.

Unbidden, a vivid memory surged to the forefront of her mind: she and Mira, years younger, laughing together in the golden light of a summer afternoon. They had been inseparable, two halves of a single soul, bound by a friendship that seemed unbreakable. But even the strongest bonds could shatter, and theirs had crumbled like sand beneath the weight of betrayal.

Elena's throat tightened as she recalled the moment everything had changed. The accusation in Mira's eyes, the disbelief and anger in her voice as she hurled words like weapons: "How could you? I trusted you, Elena. I trusted you with everything, and you threw it all away."

That memory haunted her, the pain as fresh as if it had happened yesterday. She had tried to explain, to make Mira understand, but the damage had been done. Their trust, once so strong, shattered like glass, leaving only jagged edges and bleeding wounds.

In the years since, Elena had built a new life shaped by the lessons learned from that bitter betrayal. She had learned to guard her heart, to keep her distance from those who might hurt her. The Ember Lounge became her refuge, a place to lose herself in work and music, where she could forget, if only for a moment, the ache that lingered in her chest.

But Mira's sudden reappearance had ripped open all

those old wounds. Elena felt familiar pain welling up inside her—the hurt, anger, and longing she had tried so hard to bury. She clenched her fists, nails biting into her palms, and forced herself to take a deep, steadying breath.

She couldn't let herself be thrown off balance now. She had worked too hard, come too far, to let the ghosts of her past drag her back down. Whatever Mira's reason for being here, Elena would face it with the same strength and determination that had carried her through the trials of recent years.

With a final, calming exhalation, Elena straightened her spine and squared her shoulders. She smoothed the wrinkles from her blouse, tucked a stray lock of hair behind her ear, and fixed her features into a mask of cool professionalism. Then, with one last glance around her office, she turned and step

* * *

The shrill ring of the phone cut through the low hum of conversation and clinking glasses, jolting Elena from her thoughts. She reached for the receiver, the cool plastic a welcome anchor to the present moment. "Ember Lounge, this is Elena speaking."

The voice on the other end of the line was familiar, the cadence of the words a well-worn groove in her mind.

"Elena, it's Jack from Solstice Distributors. I wanted to confirm the delivery schedule for next week."

She cradled the phone between her ear and shoulder, reaching for a pen and notepad. "Of course, Jack. Let me just pull up the order." Her fingers flipped through the pages, the rustling of paper a soothing counterpoint to the thrum of her heartbeat. "Looks like we're expecting the shipment on Tuesday morning, around 10 AM."

"That's right," Jack confirmed, his voice tinged with a hint of admiration. "You always were one for the details, Elena. It's no wonder The Ember Lounge is doing so well."

A small smile tugged at the corners of her lips, a flicker of pride sparking in her chest. "I do my best, Jack. This place is my life."

As she jotted down the final notes, her gaze drifted across the room, taking in the sea of faces, the ebb and flow of bodies. And then, like a lightning bolt, her eyes locked onto a familiar figure, the sight sending a jolt of electricity down her spine.

Mira.

She was here, standing at the edge of the bar, her eyes fixed on Elena with an intensity that stole the breath from her lungs. The world around her faded away, the sounds of the bar muffled and distant, as if she were underwater. Her heart raced, a staccato rhythm that pounded in her ears, and her grip tightened on the phone, the plastic creaking under the pressure.

"Elena? Are you still there?" Jack's voice filtered through the haze, a lifeline back to reality.

She blinked, tearing her gaze away from Mira's magnetic pull. "Yes, sorry, I'm here. Tuesday at 10 AM. Got it."

As she ended the call, she could feel the weight of Mira's stare, the heat of it searing her skin. Her palms were slick with sweat, and she wiped them surreptitiously on the fabric of her pants. She knew she couldn't avoid this confrontation forever, but the thought of facing Mira, of dredging up the pain and betrayal of their past, made her stomach churn with dread.

She took a deep breath, steeling herself for the inevitable. She was Elena Martinez, and she would not be cowed by the ghosts of her past. With a final glance at Mira, she straightened her shoulders and stepped out from behind the bar, ready to face whatever came next.

Two

THE SOUND of Chloe's laughter drifted into the bedroom, pulling Mira from slumber. A smile curved her lips as she blinked awake, morning light filtering through gossamer curtains. Warmth bloomed in her chest, radiating like the first rays of dawn.

She slid from beneath the covers and padded down the hallway, the cool hardwood floors beneath her bare feet. Chloe's giggles grew louder as Mira neared the kitchen. Leaning against the doorframe, she savored the sight of her daughter—golden hair tousled, cherubic face alight with glee as she played with her stuffed bunny at the table.

"Morning, sunshine," Mira said softly.

Chloe's head whipped around. "Mommy!" She launched herself into Mira's arms.

Mira held her tight, breathing in the sweet scent of no-tears shampoo and fabric softener lingering on Chloe's pajamas. For a moment, everything felt right in the world.

Reluctantly, she released Chloe and turned to the stove. Whisking eggs, she added a splash of milk, salt, and pepper. The pan sizzled as she poured in the mixture, tendrils of steam curling in the air. The aromas of butter and warming bread mingled as she slid slices into the toaster. She flipped the eggs with a practiced flick of her wrist, golden layers flecked with herbs.

Simple pleasures, Mira mused as she plated the fluffy eggs alongside crisp triangles of toast glistening with melted butter. She grabbed Chloe's favorite strawberry jam from the fridge, a splurge from the farmer's market last weekend.

"Breakfast is served, my lady," she announced with a playful bow, setting the plate before Chloe.

"Thank you!" Chloe sang, already reaching for her fork.

As her daughter dug in, Mira leaned back against the counter, sipping her coffee. She wanted to suspend this pocket of tranquility in their sunlit kitchen.

But shadows lingered at the edges of her mind—echoes of choices made and chances lost. Mira understood how quickly the tides could shift, sweeping away any illusion of solid ground.

Shaking off the melancholy, she focused on Chloe's gap-toothed grin smeared with strawberry jam, the easy joy radiating from her. Mira would move mountains to protect this—protect her. The past held only the power she granted it.

Draining the last of her coffee, Mira squared her shoulders. Whatever the day brought, she would meet it head-on. For Chloe, and for herself.

With breakfast finished, they moved through their morning routine with the synchronicity of countless repetitions. Mira braided Chloe's hair, deftly weaving the golden strands as Chloe chattered about her plans for school.

Mira listened, marveling at her daughter's boundless enthusiasm. She envied that innocence, the ability to greet each day as a blank canvas. Her own felt weighted down by the muted hues of yesterday.

As she tied off the braid with a blue ribbon, Mira caught her reflection in the hallway mirror. The weariness around her eyes and the tightness in her smile were subtle signs of the burdens she carried. But there was strength there too, hard-won and unyielding.

"Ready, Mom?" Chloe tugged at Mira's hand.

Mira nodded, grabbing her keys and ushering Chloe out the door. The crisp morning air greeted them, carrying the scent of dew-kissed grass and the distant aroma of freshly baked bread from the corner bakery.

Hand in hand, they walked through Willow Creek, the quaint houses with colorful gardens and white picket fences a picture of idyllic charm. Mira exchanged waves with neighbors tending to their rose bushes or walking dogs.

"Morning, Mira!" called Mrs. Henderson, the retired librarian. "Beautiful day, isn't it?"

"It certainly is," Mira replied, mustering a smile.

But beneath this postcard-perfect town, Mira knew currents of secrets and old wounds ran deep. She could feel them swirling around her ankles, threatening to drag her under.

Chloe skipped ahead, blissfully unaware, her laughter a bell-like peal cutting through Mira's haze of thoughts. She was the lifeline Mira clung to, the beacon guiding her back to shore.

As they approached the school, its red brick facade rose before them, and Mira's step faltered. The weight of the day ahead settled heavily on her shoulders—the promise and peril of it.

But for Chloe, she would carry on. One foot in front of the other, no matter how unsteady the ground felt.

At the school gates, Chloe turned to Mira, her green eyes wide and earnest. "Mommy, can we get ice cream after school today?"

Mira crouched down, brushing a stray curl from Chloe's forehead. "Of course, sweetheart. It's a date." She pulled her daughter into a tight hug, breathing in the sweet scent of her strawberry shampoo.

Too soon, the bell rang, and Chloe pulled away, her backpack bouncing as she ran to join her friends. At the door, she paused to wave. "Love you, Mommy!"

"Love you more," Mira whispered, her words carried away on the breeze.

She stood watching until Chloe disappeared inside, her heart a tangle of love and fear. In a world of uncertainties, her daughter was the one constant, the North Star guiding her home.

With a sigh, Mira turned away from the school, her feet carrying her down the familiar path to the bookstore. The sign above the door, "The Storyteller's Nook," greeted her like an old friend.

The scent of books enveloped her, a balm to her weary soul. Mira ran her fingers along the spines, their worn covers and dog-eared pages a testament to the power of the stories within.

"Morning, Mira!" her co-worker Sarah called from behind the counter. "I've got a fresh pot of coffee brewing in the back."

Mira managed a smile. "You're a lifesaver, Sarah. I'll be right there."

But first, she had a ritual to complete. Mira made her way to the back of the store, to the shelf where her favorite book resided—a battered copy of "To Kill a Mockingbird," the pages yellowed with age.

She cradled it in her hands, tracing the opening lines:

"When he was nearly thirteen, my brother Jem got his arm badly broken at the elbow..."

The familiar words washed over her, a momentary escape from her troubles. In the pages of a book, Mira could lose herself, finding solace and strength.

The jingle of the bell above the door pulled her back to the present. Mira shelved the book and straightened her shoulders, turning to greet the customer.

"Welcome to The Storyteller's Nook," she said, her voice warm and inviting. "How can I help you today?"

The elderly gentleman smiled, his eyes crinkling at the corners. "I'm looking for a book for my granddaughter. She's just learning to read."

Mira nodded, gesturing for him to follow. "I have the perfect selection. Right this way."

As she guided him through the stacks, Mira felt a sense of purpose settle over her. Here, among the books, she was in her element. Here, she could make a difference, one story at a time.

Yet, even as she immersed herself in her work, the ghosts of her past lingered at the edges of her mind, waiting to be confronted. For now, though, she pushed them aside, focusing on the joy of sharing her love of literature with others. It was a small victory, but one she clung to—a lifeline in a sea of uncertainty.

***

Mira glanced at her watch and realized it was time for the community project meeting at Harmony Hall. She bid farewell to her co-worker, promising to return later to help close up the bookstore. With a deep breath, she stepped into the bustling street, her mind racing with ideas for the town's development.

The short walk to Harmony Hall offered Mira a moment of introspection. She sensed that this meeting would be pivotal, though she couldn't pinpoint why. As she climbed the steps to the historic building, anticipation thrummed in her veins.

Pushing open the heavy wooden door, she was greeted by the soft murmur of voices. The meeting room was filled with familiar faces—business owners and community leaders she had come to know well over the years. She scanned the room, offering polite smiles and nods of acknowledgment.

Then her gaze landed on Elena Martinez, her former best friend and once-constant companion, now a stranger. Mira's breath caught in her throat, her heart stumbling.

Elena looked up, their eyes locking across the room. For a moment, time seemed to slow, the years melting away. Mira saw a flicker in Elena's dark eyes—surprise, perhaps, or a hint of the warmth they once shared.

But just as quickly, the moment passed. Elena's expression shuttered, her jaw tightening almost imperceptibly as she turned her attention to the papers in front of her.

Mira swallowed hard, struggling to regain her composure. She hadn't expected to see Elena here and wasn't prepared for the flood of memories and emotions that her presence unleashed.

Taking her seat, Mira's mind raced with questions—apologies and explanations she had rehearsed countless times. Yet, faced with the reality of Elena, she found herself at a loss for words.

As the meeting began, the drone of voices faded into the background while Mira focused on Elena. The tension between them crackled like an electrical current.

Mira's fingers tightened around her pen, knuckles turning white. She forced herself to breathe, pushing down the rising tide of emotion that threatened to overwhelm her.

She had come to represent the bookstore and contribute to the town's future. She couldn't let her past with Elena distract her from that purpose.

But even as she tried to focus on the discussion, her thoughts drifted back to Elena and the unresolved pain that hung between them.

With a bone-deep certainty, she knew this meeting was only the beginning. The path forward, for both the town and her heart, would be fraught with challenges.

For now, Mira clung to her composure, the façade of calm she had perfected over the years. She would face this, as she had faced every trial in her life—with quiet strength and determination.

Even if, beneath the surface, her heart was breaking all over again.

The meeting dragged on, a blur of voices and faces that Mira struggled to differentiate. She nodded at the appropriate moments and scribbled notes in the margins of her agenda, but her mind was miles away, trapped in memories she had tried desperately to forget.

* * *

Flashback

> *The sun danced on the surface of the lake, golden rays painting the water in shades of amber and bronze. Mira lay on the shore, her head resting on Elena's lap, the warmth of her skin seeping through the thin fabric of her sundress.*
>
> *"Do you ever think about the future?" Elena asked, her fingers gently combing through Mira's hair.*
>
> *Mira hummed contentedly, eyes fluttering closed. "Sometimes. But right now, all I*

can think about is how perfect this moment is."

Elena's laughter rang out, clear and bright. "You're such a sap, Mira."

"Only for you," Mira murmured, turning to press a soft kiss against Elena's palm.

The memory shifted; colors bled together, edges blurring. Suddenly, Mira found herself standing in Elena's apartment, heart pounding, hands shaking at her sides.

"How could you?" she whispered, her voice cracking. "How could you do this to me?"

Elena's face was a mask of sorrow and regret. "Mira, please. Let me explain."

But Mira was already backing away, her vision blurred by tears. "No. I trusted you. I loved you. And you betrayed me.

End Flashback

* * *

The sound of chairs scraping against the floor jolted Mira back to the present. The meeting was over, and the room was emptying around her. She blinked, disoriented, her mind still reeling from the onslaught of memories.

Slowly, she gathered her things, her movements mechanical, thoughts distant. She felt Elena's eyes on her, sensing the unspoken questions hanging in the air between them.

But she couldn't face her. Not yet. Not when the wounds were still raw, the pain still fresh.

Mira stood, her chair scraping loudly against the floor. Taking a deep breath, she squared her shoulders and turned toward the door.

Elena's gaze bore into her back as she walked away, the echo of her own footsteps reverberating against the hardwood.

But she didn't look back. She couldn't. Not when the past was still so close, so real, so impossible to escape.

* * *

Mira stepped into the hallway, her heart pounding. The

air felt thick and suffocating, as if the weight of her memories pressed down on her from all sides.

She walked quickly, footsteps echoing off the walls, her mind racing with thoughts of Elena, their past, and the future that could have been. But there was no going back—no way to undo the damage done, the trust broken.

Now, she had to think of Chloe. She needed to protect her from the heartache that came with loving someone who could hurt you so deeply.

Mira pushed open the door to the parking lot, the cool air hitting her face like a slap. She took a deep breath, trying to steady herself and push away the memories threatening to overwhelm her. But they clung to her like cobwebs, sticky and persistent, refusing to let go.

Fumbling with her keys, her hands shook as she unlocked her car. She slid behind the wheel, gripping the steering wheel so tightly her knuckles turned white. Alone in the silence, Mira let the tears come.

They streamed down her face, hot and bitter, as she mourned the love she had lost and the future stolen from her. She cried until her eyes were red and swollen, until her throat was raw.

With a shuddering breath, she wiped away her tears and started the engine. She had to keep moving forward, to find a way to make peace with her past and build a future for herself and Chloe.

As she pulled out of the parking lot, uncertainty loomed large in her mind. The road stretched before her, winding and unknown, and Mira knew the journey would be long and difficult.

But she had no choice but to take it, one step at a time, one day at a time. With a heavy heart and determined spirit, Mira drove into the gathering dusk, ready to face whatever challenges lay ahead.

Three

ELENA STEPPED INTO HARMONY HALL, the click of her heels against the polished wood floor blending into the murmur of voices and clink of glasses. The air was thick with expensive perfume and decades of history. She scanned the dimly lit room, her dark eyes searching the crowd of elegantly dressed women, some vaguely familiar, others strangers.

Her heart raced as she spotted a cascade of blonde hair across the room. Mira. Even from behind, that slender frame and the tilt of her head were unmistakable. A tempest of emotions swirled inside Elena—anticipation, resentment, longing. For a moment, she was frozen, as if Mira's presence had turned the floor to quicksand beneath her feet.

Elena swallowed hard, steeling herself. She had anticipated this moment, replayed it in her mind countless times. Yet, her hands trembled as she smoothed the front of her black cocktail dress.

Get it together, she chided herself. *You didn't claw your way to success to lose your nerve now.* With a deep breath, she willed her features into a mask of cool composure and began to cross the room, the crowd parting before her like a sea.

As she drew closer, details emerged—the graceful line of Mira's neck, the way the emerald silk of her dress shimmered under the chandeliers. Elena's breath caught. God, she was still so beautiful it made her ache. Time seemed to slow as Mira turned, those sea-green eyes widening in surprise.

In that charged moment, the years fell away, and they were twenty-three again, inseparable, with a limitless future ahead. Before the betrayal that shattered their friendship and sent them on divergent paths. Before Elena built walls around her heart, vowing never to trust again.

Mira recovered first, a tentative smile curving her lips, making Elena's pulse stutter. "Elena. It's... good to see you." Her husky voice was achingly familiar.

"Hi, Mira." Elena inclined her head, fighting to keep her expression neutral, even as a storm raged inside her. "I wasn't sure you would come." The unspoken words hung between them, heavy with the weight of their shared past.

A shadow flickered across Mira's face before she

composed herself. "I almost didn't." She met Elena's gaze, unflinching. "But we both know there are things that need to be said. Wouldn't you agree?"

Elena hesitated, caught between the desire for answers and the fear of reopening old wounds. Around them, the party swirled—glasses clinking, laughter ringing out, oblivious to the silent war between two former friends.

Finally, Elena nodded slowly. "We're long overdue for a conversation." She gestured toward the bar. "Shall we get a drink first? For old times' sake." It was both a peace offering and a challenge, their history distilled into a single question.

Mira searched Elena's face for a moment before exhaling. "Lead the way." As they wove through the crowd, Elena felt the weight of Mira's presence beside her, the air crackling with tension. A small voice whispered a dangerous question: After all these years, could there still be something between them?

Elena led Mira through the throng of partygoers, acutely aware of the heat radiating from her. The scent of Mira's perfume—a familiar blend of jasmine and sandalwood—stirred memories Elena had long tried to suppress. As they approached the bar, Elena's fingers brushed against Mira's arm, sending a jolt of electricity through her.

"What can I get for you?" The bartender's voice cut

through the charged silence, grounding Elena in the present.

Mira glanced at Elena, a hint of a smile playing at her lips. "I'll have a gin and tonic, please."

Elena nodded, her voice steady despite her racing heart. "Make that two."

As the bartender prepared their drinks, Elena turned to Mira, searching for any sign of the connection they once shared. "So, how have you been? It's been... a long time."

Mira traced the condensation on her glass, her eyes distant. "Managing. Raising Chloe, running the bookstore. It keeps me busy." She paused, meeting Elena's gaze. "What about you? The Ember Lounge seems to be thriving."

Elena shrugged, taking a sip of her drink. The gin burned her throat but provided a welcome distraction. "It's been a lot of work, but worth it. The lounge is my life now."

Mira's eyes softened. "I know what that's like. Pouring everything into something, hoping it fills the void."

Elena's breath caught, the words hitting too close to home. She looked away, tightening her grip on her glass. "Mira, I—"

Before she could continue, laughter from a nearby group shattered the moment, severing the fragile connection. Elena shook her head, the walls around her heart snapping back into place. "We should probably mingle. It's a party, after all."

Mira hesitated, searching Elena's face. For a moment, it seemed she might argue, but then she nodded, expression shuttering. "You're right. We wouldn't want to draw too much attention to ourselves."

As they stepped away from the bar, drinks in hand, Elena couldn't shake the feeling that something important had slipped through her fingers. She glanced at Mira, wondering if she felt it too—the unspoken words, the lingering questions, the possibility of what could have been.

But the moment had passed, and the party swirled around them, a sea of strangers and forgotten dreams. Elena took another sip of her drink, the bitterness mirroring the ache in her heart. Tonight, she would play the role of the confident and aloof Elena Martinez. Yet, a part of her would always belong to Mira, no matter how hard she tried to deny it.

Elena scanned the room, her gaze drawn to familiar faces and laughter that filled Harmony Hall. Even as she smiled and nodded at acquaintances, her mind remained tethered to the woman just a few feet away. Mira's presence was a gravitational pull, refusing to be ignored.

Sensing Elena's stare, Mira turned, their eyes locking.

In that moment, the world faded away, leaving just the two of them suspended in a bubble of unspoken emotions and shared history. Elena's breath caught; her heart raced as she tried to decipher the flicker of something more behind Mira's guarded expression.

Was it regret? Longing? A hint of the connection they once shared before the betrayal that had torn them apart? The intensity of Mira's gaze sent a shiver down Elena's spine, awakening feelings she had long buried.

Mira's heart skipped as she took in Elena's familiar presence, memories flooding her mind—late-night conversations, shared laughter, the warmth of a friendship that had once meant everything. But those memories were quickly overshadowed by the sharp sting of betrayal that lingered.

She swallowed hard, fingers tightening around her glass as she fought to maintain her composure. Elena's presence was both a balm and a curse, a reminder of all she had lost. In those dark eyes, Mira saw her own regrets reflected, the unspoken apologies heavy in the air.

For a long moment, silence enveloped them, their gazes locked in a silent battle. It was Elena who broke the spell, her voice low as she raised her glass. "To old friends and new beginnings," she said, laced with bittersweet irony.

Mira hesitated, her lips curving into a wry smile as she

mirrored the gesture. "To second chances," she replied, her words carrying the weight of a promise she wasn't sure she could keep.

As they sipped their drinks, the party slowly came back into focus, the sounds washing over them once more. Yet, even as they turned to mingle with other guests, the fragile thread of connection between them remained, refusing to sever.

Elena lingered on Mira as she set her glass down, tracing the rim with deliberate slowness. "So, how have you been? It's been a while since we last saw each other."

Mira's heart raced at the question, memories of their last encounter flooding her mind. "I've been... managing," she replied, her words measured. "Life keeps you on your toes, doesn't it?"

A flicker of something unreadable passed through Elena's eyes. "It certainly does," she agreed, her gaze steady. "You moved back to Willow Creek recently. Aside from helping with the family business, what brought you back after all this time?"

The question hung heavy between them, weighted with unspoken implications. Mira hesitated, searching for the right words. "I needed a fresh start," she said finally, her voice barely above a whisper.

Her heart ached with memories of what they had once been, of the love they had shared and the betrayal that had torn them apart. She wanted to reach out, to bridge the gap, but fear of rejection held her back. Instead, she forced a smile, her voice light as she changed the subject. "So, how's The Ember Lounge doing these days? I heard you've been making quite a name for yourself."

Elena's shoulders tensed, the moment of vulnerability slipping away. "It's doing well," she replied, tone guarded. "Keeping me busy, as always."

Mira nodded, her own experiences as a single mother and entrepreneur all too familiar. "I do," she agreed, meeting Elena's gaze. "It's not easy balancing everything, trying to keep it all together."

For a moment, something unspoken passed between them—a shared understanding of their struggles. Elena's eyes softened, a hint of old warmth flickering within them. "No, it's not," she admitted, her voice a whisper. "But we've always been fighters, haven't we? You and me, against the world."

The words reminded Mira of their bond, of the love that had sustained them through the darkest times. She opened her mouth to speak, to give voice to the emotions threatening to overwhelm her, but laughter from across the room shattered the moment.

Elena's gaze darted away, her walls slamming back into place. "I should probably mingle," she said, her voice once again neutral. "It was good to see you, Mira. Take care of yourself, okay?"

Before Mira could respond, Elena turned away, her

hair swaying as she disappeared into the crowd. Mira watched her go, heart heavy with the weight of all that remained unspoken. This was only the beginning; there was still so much left to say and do. For now, she could only hope that the warmth she had glimpsed in Elena's eyes was a sign of healing to come.

* * *

Mira sighed, her gaze lingering on the spot where Elena had vanished into the throng. The brief encounter left her feeling raw and exposed, old wounds reopening as memories flooded back. She took a deep breath, trying to steady herself, but the scent of Elena's perfume still clung to the air—a haunting reminder of their past.

As she moved through the crowd, Mira's mind drifted to simpler times when she and Elena had been inseparable. She could picture them lying on the grass in the park, fingers intertwined as they watched clouds drift by, dreaming of future adventures. Those dreams had shattered, torn apart by Mira's choices and the secrets she had kept. She had thought she was protecting Elena, shielding her from the truth, but in reality, she had driven her away.

Mira's heart clenched at the memory of the betrayal etched on Elena's face during her confession. She had tried to explain, but the words had stuck in her throat, choked by guilt. Years later, the pain remained—a constant ache she carried daily. She had tried to move on, to build a new life for herself and Chloe, but the past had a way of catching up, no matter how far she ran.

As the night wore on, Mira found herself drawn back to Elena, her eyes searching the crowd. She watched as Elena laughed and chatted, her face a mask of charm and ease. Yet, Mira could see the cracks—a fleeting falter of her smile, a distant look in her eyes.

Mira longed to take Elena's hand, to lead her away from the noise and chaos to a place where they could finally talk. But she knew it was too soon; the wounds were still fresh, the hurt too deep. So instead, she waited, biding her time for the right moment—a reckoning to finally lay the past to rest and start anew. When that moment arrived, she would be ready, heart open and words true.

As the conversation lulled, Elena found herself unconsciously leaning closer to Mira. The air hummed with an electric current, palpable tension building between them. Elena's eyes drifted to Mira's lips, lingering there for a heartbeat too long before darting away, a flush creeping up her neck.

Mira felt the shift in the atmosphere, the room narrowing until it felt like just the two of them, suspended in a moment that stretched on for eternity. She noticed Elena's fingers fidgeting with the stem of her wine glass—a telltale sign of her nervousness. The urge to reach out and still those restless hands was almost overwhelming, but Mira resisted, knowing the slightest touch could shatter the fragile truce they had built.

Instead, she let her gaze linger on Elena's face, observing the subtle changes time had wrought. The lines around her eyes were a little deeper, the set of her jaw more determined. Yet beneath it all, she was still the same Elena Mira had known and loved. The realization hit her like a physical blow, stealing her breath.

She's still so beautiful, Mira thought, her heart aching with a bittersweet mix of longing and regret. *How did I ever let her go?*

The silence stretched between them, heavy with unspoken words. When Elena's eyes met Mira's, the rest of the world faded away. In that instant, they were no longer two strangers bound by a shared past, but two souls connected by a bond that time and distance could never sever.

The moment shattered with laughter from a nearby group, jolting them back to reality. Elena blinked, her expression shuttering as she stepped back, creating a careful distance between them. Mira felt the loss like a physical ache, but she knew it was necessary; they both needed time to process the emotions stirred by their unexpected reunion.

As the chapter drew to a close, Elena and Mira stood facing each other, the air crackling with tension and possibility. The future stretched out before them, uncertain and uncharted, but one thing was clear: their story was far from over. With a final, lingering look, they parted ways, each carrying the memory of that charged moment—a promise of what could be, if only they were brave enough to reach for it.

Four

THE EMBER LOUNGE pulsed with energy as the weekend crowd filled the dimly lit space. Behind the polished mahogany bar, Elena Martinez moved with practiced precision, her hands a blur as she wiped down glasses and arranged them in neat rows. Beside her, Harper Davis mixed a vibrant blue cocktail, their movements perfectly synchronized after years of working side by side.

Elena's dark hair swayed as she reached for another glass, the phoenix tattoo on her shoulder peeking out from beneath her black tank top. She focused intently on the task, determined to keep the bar running smoothly despite the rush. Yet, her thoughts drifted to Mira, a familiar ache settling in her chest.

Harper glanced over, her hazel eyes sparkling with mischief as she garnished the electric blue drink with a slice of lime. "Another Sapphire Siren coming right up!" she announced, sliding the cocktail across the bar to a waiting patron.

Elena managed a small smile, though it didn't reach her guarded eyes. She appreciated Harper's unwavering optimism, even amidst the packed lounge, thick with scents of perfume and spilled beer.

Sensing Elena's somber mood, Harper bumped her hip playfully. "Hey, brighten up, boss lady. The night is young, and the tips are flowing!"

Elena rolled her eyes good-naturedly. "Easy for you to say. You thrive on this chaos."

Harper laughed, her curly red hair bouncing. "Damn right I do. There's nothing like the thrill of slinging drinks and making connections." She winked before mixing another colorful concoction.

Elena envied Harper's easy confidence, the way she navigated life with vibrant fearlessness. Elena had built walls around her heart, fortified by betrayal and loss, terrified of letting anyone get too close again—especially Mira.

The clinking of glasses and raucous laughter filled the lounge, but Elena barely noticed, caught up in her tangled emotions. She glanced at Harper, wondering how different things might be if she could embrace her friend's carefree approach. If she could find the courage to tear down her defenses, brick by brittle brick.

But the thought of lowering her guard sent a shiver

down her spine. She had sacrificed too much to risk it all on the fickle nature of affection, even if her heart whispered that Mira was worth the gamble.

As if drawn by an invisible thread, Elena's gaze drifted to the front door, half-expecting Mira to appear like a ghost from her past. But the entrance remained empty, filled only with eager patrons ready to drown their sorrows.

With a sharp inhale, Elena tore her attention back to the task at hand. She had a bar to run and customers to serve. There would be time to untangle the knots in her heart later, in the solitude of her apartment above the lounge. For now, she needed to keep moving forward, one glass at a time, despite the weight of her past.

Beside her, Harper continued to mix drinks with effortless flair, her laughter ringing out above the crowd. Drawing strength from her friend's irrepressible spirit, Elena found comfort in their shared rhythm. Together, they weathered the storm of thirsty patrons, a well-oiled machine forged in their unbreakable bond.

As the night wore on and the crowd began to thin, Elena allowed herself a moment to breathe, to savor the fleeting sense of peace settling over the lounge. She knew it wouldn't last—but for now, she let herself bask in the familiar rhythm of clinking glasses and Harper's comforting presence. Tomorrow would bring fresh challenges and old wounds, but tonight, she had this. And for a brief, shining moment, it was enough.

* * *

Elena polished the glasses until they sparkled under the dim lights of the lounge. The repetitive motion soothed her, allowing her mind to drift to the one topic she'd been trying to avoid: Mira.

"I saw her today," Elena murmured, her voice barely audible over the hum of conversation and the clink of ice in Harper's shaker. "At the grocery store."

Harper paused mid-pour, her vibrant eyes softening with understanding. "And how did that go?"

Elena shrugged, her gaze fixed on the glass in her hands. "About as well as you'd expect. We exchanged awkward pleasantries, danced around the elephant in the room." She sighed, her shoulders sagging under the weight of unspoken regrets. "Every time I see her, it's like no time has passed at all."

Harper reached out, brushing Elena's arm in a gesture of comfort. "That kind of history doesn't just disappear overnight. You and Mira... it was special."

Elena's throat tightened, tears pricking at the corners of her eyes. "But it ended badly. How do you come back from that? What if it's too late?"

Harper's smile was soft but reassuring. "Oh, Elena. It's

never too late for love. Not if it's the real deal." She leaned in closer, her voice dropping to a conspiratorial whisper. "From what I've seen, what you and Mira have? It's as real as it gets."

Elena's heart fluttered with a fragile hope. Could Harper be right? Could there still be a chance for her and Mira?

She opened her mouth to respond, but the words caught in her throat. Sensing her struggle, Harper gave her arm a gentle squeeze. "Just think about it. Don't let fear keep you from something amazing."

Elena nodded slowly, her mind churning with the weight of Harper's words. She knew her friend was right; the only thing holding her back was her own stubborn pride and past scars.

Beneath the fear, a spark of courage flickered to life. Maybe it was time to take a leap of faith, to trust in the power of second chances.

She glanced up at Harper, a small smile tugging at her lips. "Thanks for always knowing what to say."

Harper grinned, mischief dancing in her eyes. "That's what friends are for. Now, let's get back to work before these thirsty customers revolt."

With that, they fell back into their rhythm, the weight of the moment dissipating amidst their shared laughter and the comforting bustle of the lounge. But even as Elena immersed herself in her work, Harper's words lingered, a quiet promise of hope.

Elena moved on autopilot, wiping down the bar, but her thoughts were far away, tangled in memories of Mira. The sting of betrayal twisted in her heart, but beneath the pain lay a flicker of longing—what could have been, and what still could be if she dared to reach for it.

Harper's voice broke through her reverie. "Elena, I know you're scared. But you can't let that stop you from taking a chance on love."

Elena's fingers tightened around the rag, her knuckles turning white. "It's not that simple. Mira and I... we have a lot of history."

"And that's exactly why you need to give this a shot," Harper replied, her tone firm yet kind. "You two have something worth fighting for. Don't let pride or fear get in the way."

Elena sighed, knowing Harper was right, but the thought of vulnerability terrified her.

Sensing her hesitation, Harper covered Elena's hand with her own. "Look at me. You are one of the strongest women I know. If anyone can make this work, it's you."

Elena swallowed hard, her eyes burning with unshed tears. Harper's words settled into her heart like a balm. Maybe it was time to trust in love, even in the face of fear.

"Okay," she whispered, her voice rough with emotion. "I'll try."

Harper's face split into a wide grin. "That's my girl! Now, let's show these folks what we're made of."

Elena nodded, a small smile playing at her lips. As she mixed drinks and bantered with customers, a new sense of purpose took root within her—a determination to face her fears and fight for the love she knew she deserved.

As the night wore on, laughter and music swelled around her, and Elena felt a flicker of hope blooming in her chest. A hope for a future where she and Mira could find their way back to each other, stronger than ever before.

* * *

As the night wore on and the crowd at The Ember Lounge thinned, Elena found herself absentmindedly wiping the same spot on the bar. Harper's words echoed in her mind.

"You've got this, Lena," Harper said softly, placing a hand on Elena's shoulder. "Don't let fear hold you back from something amazing."

Elena looked up, gratitude and uncertainty shining in her eyes. "I know," she whispered. "What if she doesn't feel the same way? What if I risk everything for nothing?"

"You'll never know unless you try," Harper replied firmly. "Even if it doesn't work out, at least you'll know you had the courage to go after what you wanted."

Elena nodded, her gaze drifting to the polished wood. Harper was right, but the thought of putting her heart on the line still terrified her. She had been hurt before, watching the person she loved walk away without looking back.

But this was different. This was Mira.

The same Mira who had once been her best friend and confidante, the one who had broken her heart years ago. Yet despite everything, Elena felt an undeniable pull toward her—a magnetic force that drew her in.

Taking a deep breath, she steeled herself. "Thank you, Harper," she said, her voice soft but resolute. "I don't know what I would do without you."

Harper grinned and pulled Elena into a tight hug. "That's what friends are for. Now go get your girl. And don't forget to call me with the juicy details!"

Elena laughed, tension easing as she hugged Harper back. "I will," she promised, grabbing her jacket from the hook behind the bar. "Wish me luck."

Stepping out into the cool night air, her heart raced with a mix of fear and exhilaration. She didn't know what the future held, but for the first time in a long time, she was ready to find out.

Five

AS THE SOFT murmur of voices faded, the community leader cleared his throat. "Tonight, we'll discuss the proposed hours of operation for local businesses, particularly the new children's reading program at Mira's bookstore and its impact on Elena's bar."

Elena's heart raced. She glanced at Mira, who sat with her arms crossed and a frown etched on her face. The mention of the reading program seemed to tighten the air between them, a palpable tension making Elena's palms sweaty.

"Elena, would you like to share your thoughts?" the leader asked, gesturing toward her.

Elena hesitated, her throat dry. She could feel Mira's eyes on her, an unspoken challenge hanging between them. "Um, yes. I think we need to consider both establishments," she began, striving for steadiness. "Mira's bookstore is vital for our community, especially for families, but my bar serves as a social hub for adults. We can't dismiss the value of either."

Mira shifted in her seat, her expression hardening. "But having children around while alcohol is served could be problematic," she interjected, her tone sharp. "If my reading program is going to succeed, we need to ensure parents feel comfortable bringing their kids."

Tension thickened the air as murmurs of agreement and dissent filled the room. Elena felt a mix of anger and hurt. "I'm not suggesting we endanger anyone, Mira. Can't we find a balance? Maybe we could adjust our hours so the reading sessions don't overlap with peak bar times?"

Mira's brow furrowed, her voice rising slightly. "And what about the impact on my business? You know how hard I've worked to establish the bookstore. It feels like you're prioritizing your bar over my efforts to create a safe space for families."

Elena flinched at the accusation, the sting of Mira's words cutting deeper than she expected. "This isn't just about either of us; it's about the community! We both want what's best, don't we? What happens to kids if they don't have a safe place to read? And what about the adults who rely on the bar for socialization?"

Mira looked away, frustration palpable. "Maybe we have different ideas of what 'best' means," she murmured, her voice barely audible. "Your bar represents nightlife, while my bookstore nurtures the next generation. Those priorities don't always align."

As the meeting continued, Elena felt the divide between them widening. Each exchanged word felt like a brick added to a wall built on misunderstandings and hurt.

When the discussion shifted to other topics, Elena's mind raced. She had come hoping to reconnect with Mira, but they seemed to be drifting further apart. The ache in her chest deepened, leaving her to wonder if they could ever find common ground again.

* * *

Mira scoffed, her green eyes glittering with anger and a hint of regret. "Have you really changed, Elena? Or are you still the same selfish, manipulative girl willing to sacrifice everything for her own gain?"

The accusation hung heavy in the air, pressing down on Elena's chest. She wanted to deny it, to lash out, but deep down, she sensed a grain of truth in Mira's words.

"I've made mistakes," Elena admitted, her voice dropping to a whisper. "But I've spent the last decade trying to atone for them. This community center—it's part of that. I want to give back."

Frustration and defiance flared in Elena as Mira's

words echoed in the narrow hallway. The soft murmur of the ongoing meeting faded into the background, overshadowed by the palpable tension between them.

"How dare you question my motives?" Elena hissed, anger tightening her voice. "I've poured my heart into this project. You have no right to diminish my efforts."

Mira's eyes narrowed, meeting Elena's heated stare. A bitter laugh escaped her lips. "Spare me the righteous indignation. We both know you're no stranger to hidden agendas. Have you forgotten the betrayal that tore us apart?"

The words struck Elena like a physical blow, the air rushing from her lungs. Memories of that fateful day flooded back—pain, anger, and shattered trust, fresh and raw.

Elena clenched her fists, nails digging into her palms. She could feel the curious gazes of the other attendees, their hushed whispers a distant buzz. But in that moment, all that mattered was Mira—the woman who had once held her heart.

"That was a lifetime ago," Elena said, her voice tight. "We were young and foolish. But I've changed. I'm not the same woman I was then."

Mira remained silent, searching Elena's face for signs of deception. The tension hung thick, but as Elena met her gaze unflinchingly, a flicker of uncertainty crossed Mira's features.

"I want to believe you," Mira finally said, her voice softer but still skeptical. "But it feels like you're trying to manipulate me into a deal that benefits you, as if reconnecting is just a means to an end."

Elena stepped closer, heart pounding. "It's not like that! Yes, I want my bar to succeed, but I also want to see your bookstore thrive. We both care about this community, Mira. Can't we support each other?"

Mira's expression softened slightly, the fire in her eyes dimming. "I just don't want to be used again. I can't endure that kind of hurt a second time."

Elena nodded, understanding dawning between them. "Neither do I. But we won't know unless we talk openly. I'm trying to be better, for both of us."

For a moment, they stood in silence, charged with unspoken possibilities. Finally, Mira took a deep breath, lowering her defenses just a fraction. "Maybe we can figure this out together. But it won't be easy."

Elena offered a tentative smile, hope igniting in her chest. "I'm willing to try if you are."

As they stood in the hallway, the echoes of their argument began to fade, replaced by fragile threads of understanding weaving between them—a tentative step toward rebuilding what had been lost.

Elena stepped into the dimly lit hallway, her footsteps echoing against the polished floor. The muffled sounds of the ongoing meeting faded behind her as she moved toward the exit, her mind still reeling from the encounter with Mira.

Just as she reached for the door handle, a familiar voice called out from behind her. "Elena, wait."

The words were soft, almost hesitant, but they stopped Elena in her tracks. She turned slowly, her heart pounding as she met Mira's gaze. The other woman stood a few feet away, arms wrapped around herself as if seeking comfort.

"Mira," Elena breathed. "I thought you'd left."

Mira stepped closer, searching Elena's face. "I couldn't leave things like that. Not again."

Elena swallowed hard, her throat suddenly dry. "What do you mean?"

"I mean..." Mira paused, her gaze dropping before meeting Elena's again. "I'm tired of running away from this, from us. I know we can't erase the past, but maybe we can find a way to move forward."

Elena's heart soared at Mira's words, a flicker of hope igniting within her. She took a tentative step forward, closing the distance. "I'd like that," she murmured, her voice thick with emotion. "More than you know."

Mira's lips curved into a small smile, her eyes glistening with unshed tears. She reached out, her fingertips brushing against Elena's hand. The touch sent a shiver down Elena's spine.

"Maybe we could start with coffee?" Mira suggested,

her voice soft and hopeful. "Somewhere neutral, where we can talk without the baggage of the past weighing us down."

Elena nodded, her smile mirroring Mira's. "I'd love that. Come to my place."

As they stood in the hallway, the world around them seemed to fade away. For a moment, it was just the two of them, lost in each other's eyes, the promise of a new beginning hanging in the air.

Elena knew the road ahead wouldn't be easy—there were still wounds to heal and trust to rebuild. But as she looked at Mira, she saw a glimmer of the woman she had once loved, the woman she had never truly stopped loving.

For the first time in years, Elena allowed herself to hope that maybe, just maybe, they could find their way back to each other.

* * *

Elena stood in her cozy living room, the familiar scent of coffee mingling with the crisp autumn air wafting through the open window. Outside, the park buzzed with children's laughter, a soothing balm that drifted in like a gentle reminder of joy. She glanced at the window facing Mira's bookstore—a vibrant space filled with colorful signs and the promise of stories waiting to be told.

"I'm not asking for forgiveness, Mira. I know I have to

earn that. But can we at least call a truce? For the sake of Harmony Hall and our community?" Elena's voice was steady, though her heart raced with the weight of her words.

Mira's shoulders sagged, the burden of their shared history pressing down on her. She closed her eyes for a moment, gathering her thoughts before opening them again to meet Elena's earnest gaze. "A truce..." Her voice was barely a whisper, almost lost in the warm light of the room. "I suppose we can manage that. For the project."

Elena's heart leaped. It was a start—a fragile bridge spanning the chasm of hurt and betrayal that had grown between them. As they stood there, suspended in that moment of tentative understanding, Elena noticed how the afternoon sun softened Mira's guarded expression.

"I was thinking," Elena began, shifting to a more practical note. "What if you used my lounge for special reading sessions for kids? It could be a safe place for them."

Mira raised an eyebrow, surprised. "You would trust me to host a children's event in your home?"

"Of course," Elena replied, her voice firm.

Mira hesitated, uncertainty flickering in her eyes. "It's not just about the venue, Elena. It's about trusting that things will be different this time. If we're going to do this, I need to know you're committed."

Elena nodded, determination solidifying within her. "I am committed. This project means more to me than you realize. I want to create a space where children feel safe and loved, just as much as you do."

Mira's expression softened, a glimmer of hope sparking in her gaze. "And I want my bookstore to thrive, to be a place where families feel welcome. If we combine our strengths, maybe we can make something special."

The atmosphere shifted as they envisioned the possibilities together. "We could arrange special reading hours when the park is busy, making it a haven for families," Elena suggested. "Your bookstore can host events to draw people in, while my bar offers family-friendly activities."

Mira smiled, warmth returning to her eyes. "Exactly! And if we coordinate our schedules, we can avoid overlapping events."

A wave of relief washed over Elena. It wasn't a promise of happily ever after, but it was a beginning—a chance to heal the wounds of their past and forge a new path. "One step at a time, then?" she proposed.

"One step at a time," Mira echoed, her voice filled with cautious optimism.

As they stood in Elena's living room, surrounded by laughter from the park and the promise of new beginnings, Elena allowed herself to hope. They were no longer just two women bound by a painful history; they were allies ready to build something beautiful together.

"I want to believe you, Elena," Mira said, her voice soft

and tinged with sadness. "But how can I trust you? How can I be sure this isn't just another one of your games?"

Elena drew a shaky breath, her heart pounding. This was the moment of truth, the chance to lay her cards on the table.

"You can't," she admitted softly. "You can't be sure. But all I can do is show you, day by day, that I'm not that person anymore. That I want to make amends for my past mistakes."

She stepped closer, closing the distance until they were mere inches apart. Elena could feel Mira's warmth, the faint scent of her perfume—a reminder of the years gone by.

"Give me a chance, Mira," she whispered, emotion thick in her voice. "Let me prove I've changed, that I'm worthy of your trust again. I know I don't deserve it, but I'm asking for it anyway because I want to make things right between us."

Mira was silent for a long moment, her gaze locked with Elena's, the seconds stretching out like hours. Finally, she sighed, her shoulders dropping as if a weight had lifted. "Okay," she said softly. "I'll give you a chance. But Elena, if you hurt me again..."

Elena shook her head vehemently, her eyes shining with unshed tears. "I won't. I promise, I won't let you down, Mira. Not this time."

As they stood there, a fragile hope blossomed in

Elena's chest—a tiny spark amid the darkness of their shared past. The moment felt delicate, too precious to break.

Elena reached out, her hand hovering near Mira's arm, a silent invitation for comfort and understanding. Their eyes locked, vulnerability stretching between them. The air crackled with unspoken emotions, the ghosts of their past mingling with the faint glimmer of hope.

Mira's gaze flickered between Elena's hand and her eyes, uncertainty battling with the longing that had never truly faded. Time slowed as Mira wrestled with the decision that could change their lives.

Finally, she stepped closer, allowing her fingers to brush against Elena's—a tentative connection. The contact sent a shiver through Elena, reigniting the embers of a fire she thought had long since gone out.

"I'm scared," Mira whispered, her voice trembling. "I don't want to hurt you again. I don't know if I can trust myself not to make the same mistakes."

Elena's heart clenched at Mira's vulnerability, the raw honesty cutting through years of defenses. She curled her fingers around Mira's, a gentle anchor in the storm of emotions.

"I'm scared too," she admitted, tracing small circles on the back of Mira's hand. "But I'm tired of letting our past dictate our future."

Mira's eyes searched Elena's, a flicker of hope shining

within. "Do you really think we can start over? After everything?"

Elena smiled softly, a promise of possibility. "I think we owe it to ourselves to try. To see if we can build something new, something stronger than what we had before."

Mira's fingers tightened around Elena's, a silent agreement to face the challenges ahead together. In that moment, as the world continued to move around them, they stood still—hearts beating in sync, souls reconnecting in a dance of forgiveness and hope.

It was a small step, a tentative beginning, but enough to ignite the spark of possibility and light the way forward toward a future where their love could flourish, unbound by past mistakes.

The charged silence between them stretched on, their hands still intertwined, as if letting go would shatter the fragile connection they had just reestablished. Elena's heart raced, a heady mix of fear and exhilaration coursing through her veins. She could feel Mira's pulse beneath her fingertips, a reminder of the life and love still flowing between them.

Mira's eyes glistened with unshed tears, a testament to the depth of emotion she had kept buried. "I never meant to hurt you," she whispered, raw and trembling. "I was caught up in my own pain and fears, and I couldn't see what I was doing to you."

Elena swallowed, her own eyes stinging with the

weight of their shared history. "I know," she murmured, brushing away a stray tear down Mira's cheek. "We both made mistakes, and we let our pride and pain get in the way of what we had."

Mira leaned into Elena's touch, eyes fluttering closed for a moment, savoring the warmth. "Do you think we can find our way back? Back to what we once were?"

"I think," Elena began, her voice soft but steady, "that we first have to forgive ourselves. Let go of the guilt and anger that have held us back."

Mira nodded, a small smile tugging at her lips. "Together," she whispered, fingers tightening around Elena's.

"Together," Elena echoed, a matching smile spreading across her face.

Six

HARPER LEANED FORWARD, elbows resting on the polished bar. "So, about Mira," she began, her tone gentle yet probing. "I've noticed how you two interact, like magnets drawn to each other."

Elena's breath caught, her fingers tightening around her glass. "It's complicated," she murmured, gaze fixed on the swirling liquid.

"Love often is," Harper replied, a knowing smile on her lips. "But that doesn't mean it's not worth fighting for."

Elena's heart stuttered at the word 'love,' a concept she had long buried beneath layers of hurt. "I don't know if I can trust her again," she confessed, her voice barely above a whisper. "After everything that happened…"

Harper's hand found Elena's, her touch warm and

reassuring. "I know it's scary to open yourself up again. But I've seen how Mira looks at you. That kind of connection is rare."

Elena's mind drifted to stolen glances and lingering touches, the electricity crackling between them. "What if I'm reading too much into it?" she asked, doubt creeping in.

"You'll never know unless you take a chance," Harper encouraged, her eyes shining with earnestness. "Life is too short to let fear hold you back."

Elena's heart raced at the thought, exhilaration and terror coursing through her. The idea of baring her soul again was both thrilling and daunting. "I don't know if I'm ready," she admitted, her voice trembling. "What if I mess it up again?"

Harper's grip tightened, a fierce protectiveness radiating from her. "You won't. This time, you'll go in with your eyes wide open, with the strength you've gained from past heartbreak."

Elena drew in a shaky breath, letting Harper's words wash over her. Maybe it was time to stop running from her feelings.

"Okay," she said softly. "I'll talk to her. I'll tell her how I feel."

Harper's face lit up with a grin. "That's my girl," she said, raising her glass. "To new beginnings and second chances."

Elena clinked her glass against Harper's, a tentative smile forming. "To new beginnings," she echoed, the words a promise.

As she sipped her drink, warmth blossomed in her chest, igniting a flicker of hope.

"Thank you, Harper," Elena said, her voice thick with emotion. "I don't know what I'd do without you."

Harper squeezed her hand gently. "You'd probably be a lot less fabulous," she teased, mischief dancing in her eyes.

Elena laughed, the sound a welcome release after the heaviness of their conversation. "Probably," she agreed, her smile genuine.

Beneath the lighthearted banter, determination took root within Elena. Harper's words resonated with a truth she'd been afraid to acknowledge. She couldn't keep letting fear dictate her choices.

Thinking of Mira, of the way her green eyes made her heart skip, Elena felt the weight of regret lift. It was time to take a leap of faith.

Finishing her drink, she set the glass down with a decisive clink, meeting Harper's gaze with newfound resolve. "I'm going to tell Mira how I feel, no matter what."

Harper smiled, pride shining in her eyes. "I know you will. I'll be here for you, no matter what."

As Elena walked out of The Ember Lounge that night, the cool evening air kissed her skin. A sense of hope thrummed through her veins. The path ahead was uncertain, but for the first time in a long time, she was ready to face it head-on.

With Harper's words echoing in her mind and the memory of Mira's smile guiding her, Elena stepped into the night, determined to make her future bright.

* * *

The vibrant colors of the Harmony Hall community center greeted Elena and Mira as they stepped inside, the air buzzing with chatter and laughter. Sunlight poured through the tall windows, illuminating various art projects underway. As Elena took in the energetic atmosphere, she felt a mix of excitement and trepidation about working alongside Mira, their history looming between them.

"Welcome, ladies!" A cheerful volunteer approached, her smile wide and genuine. "We're thrilled to have you! We have the perfect task—painting a mural on the east wall. It will require collaboration, but I'm sure you'll do a fantastic job."

Elena nodded, her expression cautious. "Sounds great," Mira replied, her voice steady. "Just point us in the right direction."

As they made their way to the designated wall, Elena noticed the sunlight catching in Mira's hair, casting a soft glow. She quickly averted her gaze, focusing on the blank expanse before them. The mural design was already sketched out, featuring rolling hills and blooming wildflowers.

Elena picked up a paintbrush, dipping it into rich green paint, her movements precise. Beside her, Mira followed suit, her brush hovering over the painted flowers. They worked in silence, the gentle swish of brushes the only sound amidst the distant chatter.

Elena felt hyperaware of Mira's presence, the heat of her body inches away. It was a closeness she had once craved, now a reminder of what they had lost. As their arms occasionally brushed, a jolt of electricity surged through Elena. She gritted her teeth, trying to push aside the memories.

Despite the tension, as the mural took shape, Elena found herself stealing glances at Mira. Each detail—the furrow of her brow, the curve of her wrist—was painfully familiar yet distant. Questions burned on Elena's tongue, but she swallowed them back, focusing on the task.

The air grew heavy with unspoken words. When they stepped back to admire their progress, their gazes locked. For a fleeting moment, they were just two girls again, filled with hope and possibility. But reality crashed in; they were women shaped by their choices.

Elena's heart ached with the knowledge of all they had lost. Painting the mural was just the beginning, a tentative first step on an uncertain road. Yet, as they resumed their work, a synchronized rhythm emerged, leaving Elena to wonder if healing and forgiveness were possible.

Reaching for the deep blue paint, Elena accidentally brushed against Mira's hand. The unexpected contact startled them both, and a splash of blue landed on Mira's cheek. They stared at each other, wide-eyed, before a smile tugged at Mira's lips.

"I guess I should've been more careful," Elena said, her voice playful.

"It's not every day I get a free makeover," Mira replied, her green eyes sparkling.

Without thinking, Elena wiped the paint from Mira's cheek. The warmth of the moment spread through her. Mira's breath hitched, their gazes locked, suspended in a moment that felt both new and familiar.

As they painted, the silence between them felt lighter. Elena found herself stealing glances at Mira, marveling at the sunlight dancing across her hair.

"Do you remember," Mira began softly, "when we used to paint together as kids?"

Elena's heart clenched at the memory. "Of course. We'd spend hours in your backyard, making a mess."

Mira laughed, the sound warm. "Your mom could never stay mad at us."

They continued to paint, reminiscing about childhood adventures, sharing stories of tree houses and secret handshakes. Elena marveled at how Mira listened, her green eyes attentive, as if she could see into Elena's heart.

But Elena knew there were still hurts to address and apologies to make. For now, in this moment, she allowed herself to hope that they could find their way back to each other.

Mira dipped her brush into the blue paint. "You know, I always thought you'd make it big in the art world. Your paintings were so full of life."

Elena felt a flush at the praise. "Life had other plans. The Ember Lounge keeps me busy."

Mira nodded, understanding flickering in her eyes. "Sometimes our dreams change."

"What about you?" Elena asked gently. "Did you pursue music after we parted?"

Mira's hand stilled, and after a moment, she sighed. "No. After Chloe was born, I had to put my dreams on hold. Being a single mom didn't leave time for music."

Elena's heart ached for her. Impulsively, she laid a hand on Mira's arm. "It's never too late to pursue your passions. You're incredible, Mira. You can do anything."

Mira finally met her gaze, tears shimmering in her eyes. For a long moment, they simply looked at each other, the weight of their shared history heavy in the air.

Then Mira smiled, a small but fragile curve of her lips, holding the promise of forgiveness. "Thank you for believing in me, even after everything."

Elena squeezed her arm, acknowledging the gratitude and apology woven into Mira's words. With a deep breath, she returned to the mural, her heart lighter than it had been in years.

As they lost themselves in the act of creation, their brushstrokes synchronized, Elena felt that this moment of shared vulnerability was the first step toward healing the rift between them. Perhaps it was the beginning of something beautiful, waiting beneath layers of hurt.

Seven

AS THEY CONTINUED PAINTING, the distance between them seemed to shrink, their arms brushing against each other with increasing frequency. Elena felt a shiver run down her spine every time Mira's skin grazed hers, the brief contact igniting a spark of longing deep within her chest.

She risked a glance at Mira, only to find the other woman already looking at her, her green eyes filled with an intensity that stole Elena's breath away. In that moment, the air between them felt charged with unspoken desires, with the weight of all the things they had never dared to say.

Elena swallowed hard, her heart pounding in her chest as she forced herself to look away, to focus on the mural in front of them. But even as she dipped her brush into the paint, her mind was consumed with thoughts of Mira, of the way her lips would feel against her own, of the way her body would fit perfectly in her arms.

Suddenly, Mira let out a frustrated sigh, breaking the spell that had fallen over them. "We're out of the teal paint," she said, her brow furrowed as she stared at the empty container.

Elena blinked, her mind struggling to process the words. "What?"

"The teal paint," Mira repeated, gesturing to the mural. "We need it to finish this section, but we're all out."

Elena felt a surge of disappointment, the moment between them slipping away like sand through her fingers. But then, an idea struck her, and she felt a flicker of hope reignite in her chest.

"I think Harper might have some spare paint at The Ember Lounge," she said, her voice carefully casual. "We could go ask her if we can borrow some."

Mira hesitated, her eyes searching Elena's face for a long moment. Elena held her gaze, silently willing her to say yes, to give them an excuse to spend more time together, away from the watchful eyes of the community project.

Finally, Mira nodded, a small smile tugging at the corners of her lips. "Okay," she said softly. "Let's go."

As they set down their brushes and stepped away from the mural, Elena felt a thrill of anticipation course through her veins. She knew that this was a dangerous game she was playing, that the line between friendship and something more was blurring with every passing moment.

But as she fell into step beside Mira, their hands brushing against each other with every swing of their arms, Elena couldn't bring herself to care. All that mattered was the woman beside her, and the promise of what could be, if only they were brave enough to reach for it.

* * *

The walk to The Ember Lounge was short, but Elena savored every moment of it. The sun-dappled sidewalks and gentle breeze seemed to mirror the lightness in her heart as she and Mira engaged in easy, playful banter.

"I have to warn you," Elena said, a mischievous glint in her eye, "Harper can be a bit... enthusiastic."

Mira raised an eyebrow, a smile playing on her lips. "Enthusiastic? Should I be worried?"

Elena chuckled, shaking her head. "No, no. She's harmless. Just be prepared for a lot of questions and probably a few embarrassing stories about me."

"Oh, I can't wait to hear those," Mira teased, bumping her shoulder against Elena's.

The simple touch sent a jolt of electricity through Elena, and she had to take a steadying breath. Being this close to Mira, feeling the warmth of her presence, was intoxicating. It took all of her willpower to keep her composure, to not let the depth of her feelings show on her face.

As they approached the familiar door of The Ember Lounge, Elena felt a flicker of nervousness in her gut. Introducing Mira to Harper felt significant somehow, like she was letting her into a part of her life that she usually kept carefully guarded.

But then Mira's hand brushed against hers, a reassuring touch that seemed to say, "I'm here. You're not alone." And with that simple gesture, Elena's nervousness melted away, replaced by a sense of calm certainty.

She pushed open the door, the familiar scent of wood and whiskey enveloping them as they stepped inside. The bar was empty at this hour, save for Harper, who was wiping down glasses behind the counter.

At the sound of the door, Harper looked up, her face breaking into a wide grin when she saw Elena. But then her eyes fell on Mira, and her expression turned curious, a hint of mischief sparkling in her gaze.

"Well, well, well," Harper said, setting down the glass and sauntering over to them. "What do we have here? Elena, aren't you going to introduce me to your friend?"

Elena felt a blush creep up her neck, but she managed to keep her voice steady as she said, "Harper, this is Mira. Mira, Harper."

Mira extended her hand, a warm smile on her face. "It's nice to meet you, Harper."

Harper took her hand, shaking it firmly. "The pleasure is all mine," she said, her eyes darting between Elena and Mira. "So, what brings you two lovely ladies to my humble establishment?"

"We were hoping you might have some spare paint," Elena said, trying to ignore the knowing look in Harper's eyes. "We ran out of a color we need for the mural."

Harper's grin widened, and she winked at Elena. "Of course, of course. Anything for you, Elena. And your... friend."

The way she said "friend" made it clear that she saw right through Elena's facade, that she knew there was something more between them. Elena felt her cheeks heat up, but she forced herself to meet Harper's gaze, silently pleading with her not to say anything more.

Harper seemed to understand, because she gave a slight nod before turning to Mira. "So, Mira, tell me. How did you and Elena meet?"

As Mira launched into the story of their childhood friendship and subsequent falling out, Elena felt a wave of gratitude towards Harper. Despite her teasing, she knew that Harper would always have her back, that she would support her no matter what.

And as she watched Mira and Harper chat and laugh together, Elena felt a warmth bloom in her chest. This was what she had been missing, she realized. This feeling of connection, of belonging.

For so long, she had kept her heart carefully guarded, too afraid of getting hurt again to let anyone in. But with Mira, she felt herself starting to open up, to let down her walls brick by brick.

It was terrifying and exhilarating all at once, like standing on the edge of a cliff and looking down at the churning waters below. But as Mira's eyes met hers over Harper's shoulder, filled with warmth and understanding, Elena knew that she was ready to take the leap.

Ready to see where this journey would take her, come what may.

* * *

Elena and Mira walked back to the Harmony Hall community project, the afternoon sun casting a warm glow on their faces. The paint cans clinked softly in the bags they carried, a promise of completion hanging in the air. As they approached the mural, Elena felt a surge of anticipation, her fingers itching to bring the final touches to life.

Mira set down her bag and turned to Elena, a soft smile playing on her lips. "Ready to finish what we started?"

Elena nodded, her heart fluttering at the double

meaning behind Mira's words. She reached for a paintbrush, her hand brushing against Mira's as they began to work side by side. The world around them faded away, their movements synchronized in a dance of color and emotion.

With each stroke of the brush, Elena felt a sense of connection deepening between them. It was as if the mural was a reflection of their intertwined lives, a tapestry woven from the threads of their shared history and the promise of a future yet to be written.

As they painted, Elena found herself stealing glances at Mira, admiring the way the sunlight caught the golden strands of her hair and the concentration etched on her face. There was a serenity in her presence, a sense of calm that soothed the restless edges of Elena's soul.

Time seemed to slow, the minutes stretching into an eternity as they lost themselves in the flow of creation. Their hands moved in perfect harmony, the colors blending seamlessly under their touch. With each passing moment, the mural came to life, a testament to the power of their connection.

Finally, as the last stroke of paint was applied, Elena and Mira stepped back to admire their work. The mural was a breathtaking sight, a riot of vibrant hues and intricate designs that seemed to dance before their eyes.

But it was the look in Mira's eyes that stole Elena's breath away. Those green depths were filled with a mixture of pride, admiration, and something else—something that set Elena's heart racing and her skin tingling with anticipation.

In that moment, the tension between them became palpable, a current of electricity that crackled in the air. Elena's gaze dropped to Mira's lips, a part of her longing to close the distance between them and taste the sweetness that lingered there.

But she hesitated, the weight of their past hanging heavy in the space between them. The betrayal that had torn them apart all those years ago still cast a shadow over their newfound connection, a reminder of the fragility of trust and the scars that never truly healed.

And yet, as Mira's hand brushed against hers, a feather-light touch that sent shivers down her spine, Elena knew that she was powerless to resist the pull that drew her towards this woman. It was a force stronger than gravity, a magnetism that defied reason and logic.

She took a step closer, her heart pounding in her chest as she searched Mira's eyes for any sign of hesitation or doubt. But all she found was a reflection of her own longing, a silent invitation to take a leap of faith and see where this journey would lead them.

Around them, the Harmony Hall community project continued, the sound of laughter and conversation filling the air. But for Elena and Mira, the world had narrowed down to this single moment, a crossroads where the past and the future collided in a symphony of possibility.

And as they stood there, lost in each other's eyes, Elena knew that whatever lay ahead, she was ready to face it by Mira's side. Because in the end, it was the connection between them that mattered most—a bond that had withstood the test of time and the trials of fate, a love that refused to be denied.

Elena's heart raced as she held Mira's gaze, a thousand unspoken words hanging in the air between them. The warmth of the sun on her skin and the gentle breeze rustling through the leaves seemed to fade away, leaving only the electric current that flowed between them.

Mira's lips parted slightly, as if she wanted to say something but couldn't find the words. Elena watched as a lock of blonde hair danced across Mira's cheek, and she fought the urge to reach out and tuck it behind her ear, to feel the softness of her skin beneath her fingertips.

"Elena, I..." Mira began, her voice barely above a whisper. "I know we have a lot to talk about, but right now, I just want to..." She trailed off, her eyes flickering down to Elena's lips before meeting her gaze once more.

Elena swallowed hard, her mouth suddenly dry. She knew what Mira was asking, what she was offering. It was a chance to forget the past, to lose themselves in the moment and let the world fall away.

But even as her body yearned to close the distance

between them, Elena's mind whispered a warning. They had been here before, on the brink of something beautiful and terrifying, only to have it shatter in their hands.

"Mira, we can't..." Elena breathed, even as her hand reached out to brush against Mira's, their fingers tangling together. "We have to be sure this time. We have to know that we're both ready for this."

Mira nodded, her eyes shining with a mix of understanding and longing. "I know," she murmured. "But I also know that I've never felt this way about anyone else. You're the one, Elena. You always have been."

Elena's heart swelled at Mira's words, a rush of emotion threatening to overwhelm her. She knew that there were still obstacles to overcome, wounds to heal and trust to rebuild. But in that moment, with Mira's hand in hers and the promise of a future shimmering before them, Elena felt a sense of hope and possibility that she had never known before.

And as they stood there, lost in each other's eyes, the world around them faded away, leaving only the two of them and the love that had always been there, waiting to be discovered.

Eight

THE DOOR CLICKED SHUT, the sound echoing through the empty meeting room. Elena turned to face Mira, their eyes locking across the polished wooden table that stood between them like a silent guardian.

Shadows lengthened as the sun dipped below the horizon outside, casting the room in a soft amber glow. The air felt thick, weighted with unspoken words and long-buried emotions that threatened to surface.

Elena's heart thudded against her ribcage as she took a tentative step forward, her heels sinking into the plush carpet. Mira stood motionless, her green eyes watchful and wary, like a deer poised to flee at the first sign of danger.

"Mira..." Elena's voice came out huskier than she intended, barely above a whisper. "It's been a long time."

Mira's lips parted slightly, but no words came. She looked at Elena searchingly, as if trying to decipher a hidden code in her features. The silence stretched between them, taut and trembling with possibility.

Elena took another step, her body moving of its own accord, pulled by an invisible thread that had always tied her to Mira, despite the hurt, the anger, the betrayal. Her walls, so carefully constructed over the years, began to crack, hairline fractures spreading with each beat of her traitorous heart.

"I never thought we'd find ourselves here again," Elena continued, her voice steadier now. "Alone. After everything..."

She trailed off, memories flooding her mind unbidden - stolen glances across crowded rooms, whispered confessions under starlit skies, promises made and broken on tear-stained pillows. The weight of it all pressed down on her, threatening to crush the air from her lungs.

Mira finally spoke, her voice soft but edged with something raw and aching. "Elena...I..." She shook her head, blonde waves cascading over her shoulders. "What are we doing?"

The question hung in the charged space between them, demanding an answer that neither seemed ready to give. Elena's pulse raced as she closed the distance, until they were mere inches apart, close enough to feel the heat of Mira's breath on her skin.

"I don't know," Elena admitted, her gaze dropping to Mira's lips, then back up to meet those haunting green eyes. "But I'm tired of pretending. Aren't you?"

Her words were a challenge, a plea, a confession all rolled into one. Elena's hands twitched at her sides, aching to reach out and touch, to map the contours of Mira's face and relearn every curve and angle she had once known by heart.

But still, she hesitated. The chasm of their shared past yawned wide and deep, littered with sharp-edged memories that threatened to cut them both to ribbons if they dared to cross.

And yet...

The longing in Elena's chest swelled, a tidal wave cresting, ready to crash over them both and sweep away the wreckage of their history. She took a shuddering breath, steeling herself for the plunge.

"Mira..." she whispered, her voice rough with emotion. "I never stopped...I never stopped wanting you."

The words hung in the air, a live wire crackling with tension. Elena's heart raced as she waited for Mira's reaction, the seconds stretching into an eternity.

Then, slowly, tentatively, Mira lifted a hand to Elena's face, her fingertips grazing the skin of her cheek with a feather-light touch. Elena's eyes fluttered shut, a shaky breath escaping her lips at the contact.

"I know," Mira murmured, her voice thick with unshed tears. "God help me, Elena. I know."

And with those words, the last of their defenses crumbled, the walls they had so carefully erected reducing to dust in the face of the undeniable pull between them.

They stood there, frozen in the moment, as the fading light painted the room in shades of gold and shadow...two hearts on the precipice of something terrifying and beautiful and inevitable.

Mira's hand lingered on Elena's cheek, her thumb gently tracing the curve of her jawline. The air between them grew heavy, charged with an electric current that threatened to ignite at any moment. Elena's heart thundered in her chest, each beat a deafening echo of the desire coursing through her veins.

"We can't," Mira whispered, her words a desperate plea, even as her body betrayed her, swaying closer to Elena's warmth. "There's too much history, too much pain. We'll only hurt each other again."

Elena's hand came up to cover Mira's, their fingers intertwining in a dance of longing and hesitation. She searched Mira's eyes, looking for a glimmer of the connection they once shared, a spark of hope amidst the ashes of their past.

"Maybe," Elena breathed, her voice barely audible over the pounding of her own heart. "Or maybe we've finally found our way back to each other, after all this time."

Mira's breath hitched, her green eyes glistening with unshed tears. The weight of the years hung between them, a tapestry woven from the threads of their shared history, their triumphs and their mistakes, their love and their loss.

Elena's gaze dropped to Mira's lips, those soft, inviting curves that had haunted her dreams for longer than she cared to admit. The urge to lean in, to close the distance and taste the sweetness of Mira's mouth, was almost overwhelming.

But the moment stretched on, fragile and fleeting, as if the slightest movement could shatter the delicate balance they had achieved. The golden light filtering through the windows cast a warm glow across Mira's face, illuminating the flecks of hazel in her eyes and the faint freckles dusting her nose.

"I'm scared," Mira admitted, her voice trembling with the weight of her confession. "Scared of what this means, of what we could be."

Elena's heart clenched at the vulnerability in Mira's words, the raw honesty that cut through the years of silence and misunderstanding. She tightened her grip on Mira's hand, a silent promise, a lifeline in the tumultuous sea of their emotions.

"I know," Elena murmured, her forehead coming to rest against Mira's, their breaths mingling in the scant space between them. "I'm scared too. But I'm tired of running from this, from us. I want to face it, together."

The words hung in the air, a declaration and a question all at once. Mira's eyes searched Elena's, looking for the answers to the unspoken fears that haunted them both. The seconds ticked by, each one an eternity, as the world narrowed to the two of them, standing on the precipice of a choice that could change everything.

And then, with a shuddering breath, Mira closed her eyes and let herself fall, her lips finding Elena's in a kiss that was both achingly familiar and thrillingly new. The taste of her, the softness of her mouth, the way her body melted into Elena's embrace...it was a homecoming and a revelation all at once.

As the sun dipped below the horizon, painting the sky in shades of orange and pink, Elena and Mira lost themselves in the kiss, in the promise of a future that had once seemed impossible. The ghosts of their past still lingered, but in that moment, they were nothing more than whispers on the wind, drowned out by the beating of two hearts finally finding their way back to each other.

Mira's breath caught in her throat as Elena's fingertips grazed the delicate skin behind her ear, the touch igniting a cascade of memories and emotions that threatened to overwhelm her. The air between them crackled with tension, a heady mix of longing and uncertainty that made her heart race and her knees feel weak.

She swallowed hard, trying to steady herself against the onslaught of feelings that Elena's nearness provoked. It was a battle she had fought countless times before, the desire to lean into the warmth of Elena's touch warring with the fear of opening herself up to more pain. But as she stood there, drowning in the depths of Elena's dark eyes, Mira found herself wanting to take the risk, to reach out and grab hold of the possibility that hung between them like a promise.

Elena's voice was barely above a whisper when she spoke, the words seeming to come from somewhere deep inside her, a place she had kept hidden for so long. "I've missed you, Mira. More than I ever thought possible."

The admission hung in the air, heavy with vulnerability and a longing that Mira felt echoed in her own soul. She could see the flicker of uncertainty in Elena's eyes, the way her confident exterior faltered ever so slightly as she laid her heart bare.

Mira's own voice was thick with emotion when she replied, her words a confession and a plea all at once. "I've missed you too, Elena. Every day, every moment. It's been like a constant ache, a part of me that's been missing."

She reached out, her hand trembling slightly as she cupped Elena's cheek, marveling at the softness of her skin and the way she leaned into the touch. It was a gesture of comfort and connection, a silent acknowledgment of the bond that had never truly been broken, despite the years and the hurt that lay between them.

As they stood there, lost in the intimacy of the

moment, Mira could feel the walls around her heart beginning to crumble, the defenses she had built up over the years slowly giving way to the force of the love that still burned bright within her. It was a terrifying and exhilarating feeling, the knowledge that she was stepping into uncharted territory, risking everything for the chance to find happiness with the woman who had always held her heart.

But even as the doubts and fears swirled within her, Mira knew that she couldn't turn back now. Not when Elena was looking at her with such raw honesty, such open desire. Not when every fiber of her being was crying out to be held, to be loved, to finally find the peace and belonging that had eluded her for so long.

So she took a deep breath, steadying herself against the tide of emotions that threatened to sweep her away, and leaned in closer, her forehead coming to rest against Elena's as she whispered the words that had been burning inside her for years.

"I want this, Elena. I want us. I'm tired of living in the past, of letting my mistakes and regrets control me. I want to build a future with you, to find out what we could be together."

Elena's heart raced as Mira's words washed over her, igniting a spark of hope that had long been dormant. The air between them crackled with tension, the weight of their shared history and the promise of a future yet to be written hanging heavy in the silence.

With a shaky breath, Elena reached out, her fingers trembling as they brushed against Mira's cheek. The contact sent a shiver down her spine, a reminder of the power that Mira still held over her, even after all these years.

"I want that too," she whispered, her voice thick with emotion. "I've spent so long trying to convince myself that I was better off without you, that I could build a life on my own. But the truth is, I've never stopped loving you, Mira. I've never stopped wanting you."

The words hung in the air between them, a confession that could no longer be denied. Elena's heart hammered in her chest as she waited for Mira's response, every nerve in her body alive with anticipation.

Mira's breath caught in her throat, her pulse quickening at the feel of Elena's touch. The sincerity in Elena's eyes, the raw vulnerability in her voice, it all served to chip away at the walls Mira had so carefully constructed around her heart.

She leaned into Elena's touch, savoring the warmth of her skin, the tenderness of her caress. In that moment, the years of hurt and misunderstanding seemed to melt away, replaced by a sense of rightness, of inevitability.

"I love you too, Elena," Mira breathed, the words tumbling from her lips like a prayer. "I always have. And I know that we have a lot to work through, a lot of baggage to unpack. But I'm willing to try, if you are."

Elena nodded, a soft smile playing at the corners of her mouth. "I'm all in, Mira. No more running, no more hiding. I want to face this, together."

The tension between them reached a fever pitch, the air electric with possibility. Elena took a step forward, closing the distance between them until their bodies were mere inches apart. She could feel the heat radiating off of Mira's skin, could smell the faint scent of her perfume, could see the flecks of gold in her green eyes.

The world around them faded away, the only thing that mattered was this moment, this connection. The past and the future blurred together, the present crystallizing into a single, perfect point of clarity.

They hovered on the precipice, teetering on the edge of something profound and life-altering. The anticipation was a living thing, pulsing between them like a heartbeat, urging them forward, daring them to take the leap.

Mira's hand trembled as she reached out, her fingertips grazing the soft skin of Elena's cheek. The touch was feather-light, a whisper of sensation that sent shivers racing down Elena's spine. Mira's eyes were filled with a tender reverence, a vulnerability that took Elena's breath away.

Elena leaned into the caress, her eyes fluttering closed as she savored the warmth of Mira's touch. It was a balm to her battered soul, a soothing salve that eased the ache of the years they'd spent apart. In this moment, nothing else existed but the two of them, cocooned in a bubble of intimacy and longing.

Elena's heart pounded in her chest, a staccato rhythm that echoed the pulsing desire thrumming through her veins. She could feel the heat of Mira's body, the electricity that crackled between them, the magnetic pull that drew them ever closer. It was a force beyond her control, a gravitational tide that swept her along in its wake.

Mira's thumb brushed the corner of Elena's mouth, tracing the curve of her lower lip with a delicate touch. Elena's breath hitched, her lips parting of their own accord, an invitation and a plea all in one. She ached to close the distance between them, to taste the sweetness of Mira's kiss, to lose herself in the depths of her embrace.

But even as the desire surged within her, Elena felt a flicker of hesitation, a whisper of doubt that made her pause. The wounds of the past were still raw, the scars of betrayal not yet fully healed. Could they really move forward, after everything that had happened between them? Could they build something new and beautiful from the ashes of their broken relationship?

As if sensing her uncertainty, Mira leaned forward, resting her forehead against Elena's. "I know it won't be easy," she murmured, her breath warm against Elena's skin. "But I'm willing to fight for this, for us. I won't let my mistakes define our future, not anymore."

Elena's heart swelled with a fierce, protective love. She knew that Mira was right, that the road ahead would be a rocky one. But in this moment, with Mira's touch anchoring her to the present, Elena felt a surge of courage, a determination to face whatever challenges lay ahead.

She reached up, covering Mira's hand with her own, twining their fingers together in a gesture of unity and solidarity. "Together," she whispered, her voice rough with emotion. "We'll face it together, no matter what."

And as they stood there, lost in each other's eyes, the world around them faded away, leaving only the two of them, bound by a love that had weathered the storms of time and circumstance, ready to face the future, hand in hand.

Their lips hovered mere inches apart, the air between them electric with unspoken desire. Elena could feel Mira's soft exhalations caressing her skin, the warmth of her breath mingling with her own. In this suspended moment, the weight of their shared history seemed to melt away, replaced by a yearning that transcended the pain of the past.

Mira's hand trembled slightly as she traced the contours of Elena's face, her fingertips leaving trails of fire in their wake. Elena's eyes fluttered closed, surrendering to the sensation, her heart pounding a staccato rhythm against her ribcage. The world narrowed to the two of them, cocooned in the intimacy of the deserted meeting room.

"Elena," Mira breathed, her voice a husky whisper. "I've wanted this for so long."

Elena's eyes opened, locking with Mira's in a gaze that spoke volumes. The green depths of Mira's eyes shimmered with a potent mix of longing and trepidation, a mirror of the emotions swirling within Elena's own heart. The air between them seemed to crackle with the intensity of their connection, the pull of their attraction an almost tangible force.

Slowly, almost imperceptibly, they gravitated towards each other, drawn by an irresistible magnetism. Elena's hands found their way to Mira's waist, pulling her closer, relishing the warmth of her body pressed against her own. Mira's fingers tangled in the silken strands of Elena's hair, a gentle caress that sent shivers cascading down Elena's spine.

Their lips were a hairsbreadth apart, poised on the cusp of a kiss that promised to redefine their relationship, to shatter the barriers they had so carefully constructed. Elena's heart raced, a dizzying cocktail of anticipation and fear coursing through her veins. She knew that this moment would change everything, that there would be no going back from this precipice.

Just as their lips were about to meet, a resounding

crash echoed from beyond the meeting room, shattering the spell that had enveloped them. They jerked apart, chests heaving, eyes wide with startled realization. The outside world came rushing back in, a harsh reminder of the reality they had temporarily escaped.

Elena took a shaky step back, her breathing ragged, her skin tingling with the memory of Mira's touch. She could see the same dazed expression mirrored on Mira's face, the same mix of frustration and unfulfilled desire. The moment had been broken, their connection severed by the intrusion of the external world.

* * *

Elena and Mira exchanged a knowing glance, a silent acknowledgment of the forces that always seemed to conspire against them. The air between them still crackled with electricity, their bodies humming with the lingering echoes of unfulfilled desire. Elena's heart ached with the weight of the moment, the bittersweet realization that their path to love was strewn with obstacles.

Mira's eyes, green and expressive, held a kaleidoscope of emotions - longing, regret, and a flicker of resignation. She took a step back, her fingers slowly slipping from Elena's grasp, leaving a trail of goosebumps in their wake. The distance between them felt like a chasm, a physical manifestation of the challenges they faced.

"It seems the universe has other plans for us," Mira whispered, her voice tinged with a wistful smile. She tucked a stray lock of blonde hair behind her ear, a nervous gesture that betrayed her inner turmoil.

Elena nodded, her own voice caught in her throat. She wanted to reach out, to pull Mira back into her arms and damn the consequences, but the weight of their history, the scars of their past, held her back. "Maybe it's for the best," she managed, the words tasting bitter on her tongue.

They stood there for a moment, suspended in a fragile bubble of understanding. The path ahead was uncertain, fraught with the ghosts of their shared history and the expectations of the world around them. Their love, so powerful and all-consuming, would have to wait, to simmer beneath the surface until the time was right.

With a shared sigh, Elena and Mira turned towards the door, their footsteps heavy with the burden of their decision. They exchanged a final glance, a bittersweet smile that held the promise of a future yet to be written. As they stepped out of the meeting room, their hearts heavy with the weight of what could have been, they knew that their journey was far from over.

The door clicked shut behind them, sealing away the remnants of their stolen moment. The Harmony Hall meeting room stood silent, a witness to the unspoken desires and the unresolved tensions that lingered in the air.

Elena and Mira walked away, their bodies still yearning for each other's touch, their minds filled with the bittersweet knowledge that their love story was just beginning, even as the world conspired to keep them apart.

As Elena stepped out into the cool evening air, she felt a renewed sense of determination coursing through her veins. The brief, charged moment with Mira had ignited a fire within her, a burning desire to fight for the love they both deserved. She glanced over her shoulder, catching sight of Mira's blonde hair shimmering under the streetlights as she walked in the opposite direction.

Elena's mind raced with thoughts of the obstacles that lay ahead, the wounds of the past that still needed healing, and the societal pressures that threatened to keep them apart. Yet, beneath the weight of these challenges, there was a glimmer of hope, a whisper of possibility that refused to be silenced.

She reached up, her fingers grazing the phoenix tattoo on her shoulder, a symbol of her own resilience and strength. Just as the mythical bird rose from the ashes, Elena knew that she and Mira had the power to rise above their past, to forge a new path together.

"This isn't the end," she whispered to herself, her words carried away by the gentle breeze. "We've come too far to give up now."

With each step, Elena felt a renewed sense of purpose, a determination to break down the barriers that stood between her and Mira. She knew that the journey ahead would be filled with challenges, with moments of doubt and uncertainty, but she was ready to face them head-on.

As she walked through the quiet streets of Willow Creek, Elena's thoughts drifted to the future she envisioned with Mira. She pictured stolen moments of tenderness, shared laughter, and the warmth of Mira's embrace. She imagined building a life together, one that celebrated their love and defied the expectations of the world around them.

Elena's heart swelled with a bittersweet mix of longing and determination. She knew that the path to their happily ever after would be winding and difficult, but she was willing to fight for it with every fiber of her being. For in the depths of her soul, she knew that Mira was worth it, that their love was a force to be reckoned with.

With a deep breath, Elena squared her shoulders and continued on her way, her steps filled with purpose and her heart filled with the unshakable belief that their love story was far from over. It was just beginning, and she was ready to write the next chapter, one word at a time.

Nine

THE WINDING GRAVEL path crunched beneath Elena's boots as she approached the cozy cottage nestled among the towering pines. Warm light spilled from the windows, casting a golden glow on the wild rose bushes that flanked the front door. Elena's heart thrummed in her chest, a mix of anticipation and uncertainty coursing through her veins. She drew in a deep breath, the crisp evening air tinged with the earthy scent of the forest and the faint aroma of wood smoke from the cottage chimney.

With a trembling hand, Elena reached out and knocked on the weathered oak door, the sound echoing in the stillness of the night. Moments later, the door swung open, revealing Grace Turner's welcoming smile. The older woman's silver hair gleamed in the soft light, her eyes crinkling at the corners as she beckoned Elena inside.

"Elena, my dear. Come in, come in," Grace said, her voice warm and inviting.

Elena stepped over the threshold, the tension in her shoulders easing slightly as the comforting warmth of the cottage enveloped her. The interior was just as she remembered - rustic and charming, with hand-woven rugs, well-worn furniture, and shelves lined with books and potted herbs. The crackling fireplace cast dancing shadows on the walls, creating an atmosphere of intimacy and secrets waiting to be shared.

"Please, have a seat," Grace said, gesturing towards a plush armchair positioned near the hearth. "Make yourself comfortable."

Elena sank into the chair, the soft fabric molding to her body as she tried to quell the butterflies in her stomach. She watched as Grace settled into the opposite armchair, the flickering firelight casting an ethereal glow on her features.

What secrets does she hold? Elena wondered, her curiosity mingling with a sense of trepidation. *And what will this revelation mean for my relationship with Mira?*

Grace leaned forward slightly, her gaze intent and filled with understanding. "I'm so glad you came, Elena. I know it couldn't have been easy, given everything that's happened between you and Mira."

Elena swallowed hard, her fingers gripping the armrests as she met Grace's eyes. "I almost didn't," she admitted, her voice barely above a whisper. "But I need to know the truth. I need to understand what drove us apart."

Grace nodded, a flicker of sadness passing over her face. "The truth can be a heavy burden to bear, but it can also set us free. And I believe it's time for you to know what really happened all those years ago..."

As Grace began to speak, the room seemed to fade away, leaving only the two women and the weight of the revelation that hung between them. Elena leaned in, her heart racing as she prepared herself for the truth that would forever change the course of her life.

* * *

The warm aroma of chamomile tea wafted through the air as Grace handed Elena a steaming mug, their fingers brushing briefly in the exchange. Elena nestled back into the armchair, the soft fabric enveloping her as she took a cautious sip, the liquid soothing her frayed nerves.

"So, tell me, Elena," Grace began, her voice gentle and inviting, "how have you been? It's been far too long since we've had a chance to catch up."

Elena's gaze drifted to the crackling fire, the dancing flames mesmerizing as she gathered her thoughts. "I've been busy with the bar, as always. It's been a welcome distraction, I suppose."

Grace studied her, a knowing glint in her eye. "And what about outside of work? Have you been taking care of yourself?"

A wry smile tugged at the corner of Elena's mouth. "You know me, Grace. I've never been one for self-care. There's always something that needs my attention."

"But you can't pour from an empty cup, my dear." Grace's words hung in the air, weighted with wisdom. "Sometimes, we need to face the things we've been avoiding to truly heal."

Elena's heart stuttered, a flicker of apprehension igniting within her. She knew where this conversation was heading, but a part of her longed to keep the wounds of the past sealed shut.

Grace leaned forward, her elbows resting on her knees as she fixed Elena with a compassionate gaze. "I know it's been difficult, Elena. Your falling out with Mira... it's left a mark on both of you."

Elena's grip tightened on the mug, the heat seeping into her palms. "She made her choice, Grace. She walked away from our friendship without a second thought."

"But what if there's more to the story than you know?" Grace's voice was soft, yet it carried an undercurrent of urgency. "What if Mira had reasons for her actions that you're not aware of?"

A bitter laugh escaped Elena's lips. "What reason

could possibly justify the betrayal I felt? The pain she caused?"

Grace reached out, placing a comforting hand on Elena's knee. "Sometimes, people make mistakes, Elena. They act out of fear, or desperation, or a misguided sense of protection."

Elena's mind raced, a kaleidoscope of memories and emotions swirling within her. The late-night conversations, the shared laughter, the unspoken connection that had once bound her to Mira—all tainted by the sting of betrayal.

"I don't know if I can forgive her, Grace." Elena's voice was barely a whisper, the admission raw and vulnerable. "I don't know if I'm ready to face the truth."

Grace squeezed Elena's knee, a gesture of unwavering support. "Forgiveness isn't about condoning what happened, Elena. It's about freeing yourself from the weight of the past. It's about opening yourself up to the possibility of healing and growth."

Elena's vision blurred, tears gathering at the corners of her eyes. She blinked them away, her gaze meeting Grace's once more. "What if the truth is more than I can bear?"

"Then we'll face it together," Grace reassured her, a gentle smile gracing her features. "You're not alone in this, Elena. You never have been."

As the weight of Grace's words settled over her, Elena felt a flicker of hope ignite within her chest. Perhaps there was a chance for redemption, for understanding, for a new beginning. And with Grace by her side, she found the courage to take the first step towards unraveling the secrets of the past.

* * *

Elena drew a deep, shaky breath, the warmth of Grace's hand on her knee a steadying presence amidst the turbulence of her thoughts. The cottage seemed to fade away, the crackling of the fireplace and the soft ticking of the clock melting into the background as Elena's focus narrowed to the revelation that hung in the air between them.

"Tell me," she whispered, her voice barely audible over the pounding of her own heart. "What happened to Mira?"

Grace's eyes softened, a flicker of sadness passing over her features. She leaned forward, her voice low and gentle, as if the words she spoke were fragile, liable to shatter if uttered too harshly. "It was the summer after you left for college, Elena. Mira... she found herself in a difficult situation. She was young, scared, and alone."

Elena's brow furrowed, a sense of unease settling in the pit of her stomach. "What do you mean?"

"Mira discovered she was pregnant."

The words hung in the air, heavy and momentous.

Elena's breath caught in her throat, her mind reeling as she tried to process the implications of Grace's revelation. Mira, her once-inseparable friend, had been carrying a secret that had the power to change everything.

"She... she had a child?" Elena's voice trembled, disbelief and shock warring within her.

Grace nodded solemnly. "A daughter. Chloe. She's the light of Mira's life."

Elena's hands shook as she raised them to her face, pressing her fingertips against her closed eyelids. A kaleidoscope of memories rushed through her mind—late-night conversations, whispered secrets, dreams shared beneath starlit skies. How had she not known? How had Mira kept something so monumental hidden from her?

Questions burned on the tip of Elena's tongue, but she found herself unable to voice them. Instead, a single, painful realization cut through the chaos of her thoughts: Mira had needed her, and she hadn't been there.

"I should have been there for her," Elena whispered, her voice thick with regret. "I should have known."

Grace's hand moved from Elena's knee to clasp her hands, her touch warm and comforting. "You couldn't have known, Elena. Mira made the choice to keep her pregnancy a secret. She thought she was protecting you, sparing you from the burden of her struggles."

Elena's heart clenched, a bitter laugh escaping her lips.

"Protecting me? By pushing me away? By letting me believe that our friendship meant nothing to her?"

"Mira was young and afraid, Elena. She made choices that she deeply regrets. But she never stopped caring for you, never stopped hoping that one day, you might find your way back to each other."

Elena's mind raced, trying to reconcile the image of the Mira she had known—vibrant, ambitious, and fiercely independent—with the revelation of a young woman facing motherhood alone. A pang of empathy pierced through the veil of hurt and anger that had shrouded her heart for so long.

"I... I don't know what to do, Grace. I don't know how to face her, knowing what I know now."

Grace squeezed Elena's hands, her gaze unwavering. "You start by listening, Elena. You give her a chance to tell her story, to explain the choices she made. And then, together, you begin to heal."

Elena swallowed hard, the path ahead seeming daunting and uncertain. But as she met Grace's eyes, she found a glimmer of hope amidst the turmoil. Perhaps, with time and understanding, the broken pieces of her past could be mended, forging a new bond from the ashes of what had been lost.

"I'll try," she whispered, her voice trembling with a mix of fear and determination. "For Mira, for the friendship we once had... I'll try."

* * *

Grace's warm hand on Elena's arm anchored her amidst the tempest of emotions swirling within. The older woman's voice, gentle yet firm, washed over her like a soothing balm. "Forgiveness, my dear, is not about forgetting the past or condoning the hurt. It's about freeing yourself from the chains of resentment and allowing room for healing."

Elena's eyes glistened with unshed tears, her guarded exterior cracking under the weight of Grace's wisdom. The revelation about Mira's past had shaken the foundations of her anger, forcing her to confront the possibility that there was more to the story than she had ever known.

"But how do I even begin?" Elena's voice wavered, raw with vulnerability. "How do I let go of the pain that's been my constant companion for so long?"

Grace's eyes softened with understanding. "It starts with a single step, Elena. A willingness to open your heart, to see beyond the hurt and glimpse the humanity in the one who caused it."

Elena's gaze drifted to the flickering flames of the fireplace, their dance mesmerizing as she contemplated Grace's words. The thought of rebuilding her relationship with Mira, of bridging the chasm that had grown between them, filled her with a mixture of trepidation and longing.

"What if I'm not ready?" she whispered, her fingers

curling into the soft fabric of the armchair. "What if the wounds are too deep, the scars too thick?"

Grace leaned forward, her presence a beacon of comfort in the dimly lit room. "Healing takes time, Elena. It's a journey, not a destination. But the fact that you're here, that you're willing to consider the possibility of forgiveness... that's a testament to your strength."

A single tear escaped Elena's eye, trailing down her cheek as she absorbed the weight of Grace's words. The revelation had cracked open a door she had long believed sealed shut, inviting her to step into the unknown territory of reconciliation.

"I don't know if I can do this alone," she admitted, her voice barely above a whisper.

Grace's hand tightened on Elena's arm, a gesture of unwavering support. "You don't have to, my dear. You have people who care about you, who will walk beside you on this path. And remember, forgiveness is as much for you as it is for Mira. It's a gift you give yourself, a chance to let go of the burdens of the past and embrace a future unbridled by resentment."

As the words settled into Elena's heart, a flicker of hope ignited within her. The road ahead seemed daunting, fraught with uncertainty and emotional landmines. But for the first time in years, she allowed herself to imagine a world where the wounds of the past could be healed, where the bond she had once cherished with Mira could be reforged in the fires of forgiveness and understanding.

With a shaky breath, Elena met Grace's gaze, a newfound determination glimmering in her tear-filled eyes. "I'll try," she murmured, her voice trembling with the weight of the decision. "For myself, for Mira... for the chance to find peace."

Grace smiled, her eyes shining with pride and affection. "That's all anyone can ask of you, Elena. And know that I'll be here, every step of the way, to guide and support you on this journey."

As the two women sat in the warm glow of the fireplace, the seeds of forgiveness took root in Elena's heart, promising a future where the wounds of the past could be mended, and the bonds of friendship, once thought lost, could be rekindled in the light of understanding and compassion.

Ten

THE CACOPHONY of voices and laughter swirled through the bustling Harmony Hall as Elena stepped inside, her heart a fluttering bird within the cage of her ribs. Warm light bathed the room, casting a glow on the faces of the attendees, their expressions alight with anticipation and camaraderie. Elena's eyes darted through the crowd, seeking the one face that haunted her dreams and memories.

She weaved through the throng of people, their chatter fading to a distant hum as her focus narrowed. The scent of perfume and the rustling of fabric brushed against her senses, but they paled in comparison to the pounding of her own heartbeat. Each step felt weighted with the burden of their shared history, the unspoken words that hung between them like a veil of mist.

And then, as if the very air had parted to reveal her, Elena spotted Mira across the room. Time seemed to slow, the world narrowing to the space between them. Mira stood near the far wall, her blonde hair cascading over her shoulders like a river of golden silk. The soft lighting cast shadows across her face, accentuating the gentle curves and angles that Elena knew so well.

Elena's breath caught in her throat, a tangle of emotions surging through her veins. The years melted away, and for a fleeting moment, she saw the Mira she had once known—the friend, the confidante, the woman who had held her heart in the palm of her hand. But the illusion shattered as quickly as it had formed, replaced by the guarded expression that now graced Mira's features.

Steeling herself, Elena took a deep breath and began to weave through the crowd with purpose. Each step brought her closer to the woman who had once been her everything, the woman whose betrayal had left an indelible mark on her soul. The air crackled with tension, thick and palpable, as if the very molecules sensed the weight of their impending encounter.

As she approached, Elena's heart hammered against her ribcage, a frantic melody that echoed in her ears. She could feel the heat of Mira's gaze, those green eyes that had once looked at her with such warmth now guarded and inscrutable. The distance between them seemed to stretch into an eternity, a chasm filled with unspoken words and unresolved emotions.

With each step, the memories flooded back—the laughter they had shared, the secrets they had whispered, the gentle touches that had ignited a fire within her soul. But those memories were tainted now, stained by the bitter sting of betrayal and the ache of loss. Elena steeled herself, her jaw clenching with determination as she closed the final distance between them.

She stood before Mira now, the air electric with the charge of their proximity. The world around them faded into a distant hum, the chatter of the crowd reduced to a mere whisper. In that moment, there was only them—two women bound by a past they could not escape, tethered by a connection that refused to be severed.

Elena's lips parted, a trembling breath escaping into the space between them. The words she had rehearsed, the carefully crafted phrases she had planned to say, evaporated like mist under the heat of Mira's gaze. Instead, she found herself lost in the depths of those green eyes, searching for a glimmer of the woman she had once known, the woman she had once loved.

The silence stretched between them, heavy with the weight of unspoken emotions. Elena's heart raced, her pulse a frantic drumbeat in her ears. She could feel the electricity crackling in the air, the tension coiling tighter with each passing second. And in that moment, as their eyes locked and the world fell away, Elena knew that this encounter would be the catalyst that would either mend their fractured bond or shatter it beyond repair.

* * *

"Elena." Mira's voice broke the silence, a soft whisper that carried the weight of a thousand unsaid words. Her eyes flickered with a myriad of emotions—uncertainty, longing, and a hint of fear. "I didn't expect to see you here."

Elena swallowed hard, her throat suddenly dry. "I couldn't miss the opportunity to be part of something so important," she replied, her words measured and cautious. "The Harmony Hall project means a lot to the community."

Mira nodded, a flicker of understanding passing between them. They had both been shaped by the trials of their past, both carried the scars of the choices that had torn them apart. And yet, here they were, standing face to face, drawn together by a shared purpose.

"I'm glad you're here," Mira said softly, her eyes searching Elena's face. "It's been a long time."

Elena felt a pang in her chest, a bittersweet ache that she had never quite been able to shake. "Too long," she murmured, her voice barely above a whisper.

The moment stretched between them, charged with the electricity of unresolved feelings and unspoken truths.

Elena's heart raced, her skin tingling with the proximity of Mira's presence. She yearned to reach out, to bridge the gap that had grown between them, but the fear of rejection held her back.

Suddenly, a voice cut through the air, shattering the intimate bubble that had enveloped them. "Elena Martinez and Mira Thompson, you've been assigned to work together on the community garden project."

Elena's eyes widened, her breath catching in her throat. The very thought of working alongside Mira, of being forced to confront the ghosts of their past, sent a shiver down her spine. She glanced at Mira, searching for a reaction, but the other woman's expression remained carefully guarded.

As they made their way towards the project coordinator, Elena's mind raced with the implications of their assignment. The Harmony Hall project had brought them together, but it was the community garden that would test the strength of their fragile truce. With each step, the tension between them grew, the unresolved feelings simmering just beneath the surface.

Elena knew that the path ahead would be riddled with challenges, both external and internal. But as she walked beside Mira, their shoulders brushing, she couldn't help but feel a flicker of hope. Perhaps, in the midst of the chaos and the uncertainty, they would find a way to mend the wounds of their past and rediscover the connection that had once burned so brightly between them.

Elena and Mira stood side by side, their eyes fixed on the sprawling plot of land before them. The community garden project loomed ahead, a daunting task that demanded their collaboration. As the project coordinator outlined their responsibilities, Elena's mind wandered, acutely aware of Mira's presence beside her.

"I'll take the lead on the planting schedule," Mira said, her voice cutting through Elena's thoughts. "If that works for you."

Elena's gaze snapped to Mira, surprised by the olive branch extended in her direction. "Sure," she replied, her tone measured. "I can handle the irrigation system and coordinate with the volunteers."

Mira nodded, a flicker of relief crossing her features. They set to work, the silence between them filled with the rustling of papers and the distant chatter of the other volunteers.

As the hours ticked by, Elena found herself stealing glances at Mira, watching as she meticulously planned the garden layout. The way Mira's brow furrowed in concentration, the gentle curve of her lips as she sketched out the design—it all felt achingly familiar, stirring up memories Elena had long tried to suppress.

"What do you think about placing the tomatoes here?" Mira asked, her green eyes meeting Elena's.

Elena stepped closer, her heart racing as she leaned over the plans. The scent of Mira's perfume, a delicate blend of jasmine and vanilla, filled her senses, igniting a longing she had desperately tried to bury.

"I think that's a good idea," Elena managed, her voice barely above a whisper. "It'll get plenty of sunlight there."

Their hands brushed as they both reached for the pencil, a jolt of electricity passing between them. Elena's breath hitched, her skin tingling from the contact. She pulled back, her eyes darting away as she tried to regain her composure.

What am I doing? she thought, her mind reeling. *I can't let myself fall into this trap again.*

But as the day wore on and they continued to work side by side, Elena found herself drawn to Mira in ways she couldn't explain. The animosity that had once consumed her began to melt away, replaced by a growing desire to understand, to heal, to reconnect.

Mira, too, seemed to be fighting an internal battle. Her guarded exterior cracked, revealing glimpses of the vulnerability beneath. In the moments when their eyes met, Elena could see the unspoken questions, the yearning for closure, the hope for a second chance.

As the sun began to set, casting a golden glow over the garden, Elena and Mira stood back, admiring their progress. The once barren plot of land now held the promise of growth, of new beginnings.

"We make a good team," Mira said softly, her eyes meeting Elena's.

Elena's heart skipped a beat, the words hanging in the air between them. "Yeah," she replied, her voice thick with emotion. "I guess we do."

And in that moment, as the last rays of sunlight danced across their faces, Elena felt a flicker of hope. Hope that perhaps, in the midst of the chaos and the uncertainty, they could find their way back to each other, one garden at a time.

Elena's fingers brushed against Mira's as they reached for the same trowel, the unexpected contact sending a jolt of electricity through her body. She pulled her hand back quickly, her heart racing as she tried to regain her composure. Mira's eyes widened, a flicker of surprise and something else—something deeper—crossing her face before she looked away.

"I'm sorry," Elena murmured, her voice barely above a whisper. She busied herself with the seedlings, trying to ignore the way her skin tingled where Mira's touch had lingered.

Mira cleared her throat, her words measured and careful. "It's okay. We should probably call it a day anyway. It's getting late."

Elena nodded, not trusting herself to speak. As they cleaned up their tools and prepared to leave, the silence stretched between them, heavy with unspoken words and unresolved emotions.

Why did I react like that? Elena wondered, her mind reeling. *It was just an accident, a simple touch. But why did it feel so... electric?*

She risked a glance at Mira, only to find her already looking back, her green eyes intense and searching. For a moment, Elena felt exposed, as if Mira could see straight into her soul, into the depths of her heart where she had buried her true feelings for so long.

"Elena..." Mira began, her voice soft and hesitant. "I... I know we have a lot to work through, but I just want you to know that I..."

She trailed off, her words hanging in the air, unfinished and heavy with meaning. Elena's heart pounded in her chest, a mix of fear and anticipation coursing through her veins.

What is she trying to say? Elena wondered, her mind racing with possibilities. *Does she feel it too? This connection between us, this pull that seems to defy all logic and reason?*

But before Mira could continue, a loud commotion erupted from the other side of the garden, shattering the moment. Elena turned to see a group of volunteers arguing heatedly, their voices rising above the tranquil sounds of nature.

"We should go see what's happening," Mira said, her expression unreadable as she turned away from Elena.

Elena nodded, her heart sinking as she watched Mira walk away, the moment of vulnerability slipping through her fingers like sand. She took a deep breath, trying to calm her racing thoughts as she followed Mira towards the commotion.

Whatever this is between us, it's not going to be easy, Elena thought, steeling herself for the challenges ahead. *But maybe, just maybe, it's worth fighting for.*

As they approached the arguing volunteers, Elena couldn't shake the feeling that something had shifted between her and Mira, that the walls they had built around their hearts were beginning to crumble. And despite the uncertainty, despite the obstacles that lay ahead, she felt a flicker of hope, a glimmer of possibility that maybe, just maybe, they could find their way back to each other.

Elena's heart pounded in her chest as she followed Mira into the empty conference room, the tension crackling between them like an electrical current. The door clicked shut behind them, sealing them off from the bustling chaos of the Harmony Hall project.

Mira turned to face Elena, her green eyes flickering with a mix of apprehension and determination. "We need to talk," she said, her voice steady despite the tremor in her hands.

"Do we?" Elena asked, her own voice edged with a hint

of bitterness. "I thought we'd said everything we needed to say years ago."

Mira flinched at the barb, but she held her ground. "I know I hurt you, Elena. I know I made mistakes. But I'm not the same person I was back then."

Elena scoffed, crossing her arms over her chest as she leaned back against the conference table. "And why should I believe that? Why should I trust you after everything that's happened between us?"

"Because I'm here, aren't I?" Mira said, taking a step closer to Elena. "Because despite everything, despite the hurt and the anger and the years of silence, I still care about you. I still..."

She trailed off, her words hanging in the air between them like a confession. Elena swallowed hard, her heart hammering against her ribcage as she met Mira's gaze.

"You still what, Mira?" she asked, her voice barely above a whisper.

Mira closed the distance between them, her hands coming up to cup Elena's face. "I still love you," she breathed, her lips hovering just inches from Elena's. "I never stopped loving you."

Elena's breath caught in her throat, her eyes fluttering closed as she leaned into Mira's touch. *This is insane,* she thought, even as her body thrummed with desire. *We can't do this. We can't go down this road again.*

"Mira," she whispered, her hands coming up to tangle in the other woman's hair. "We can't..."

But Mira silenced her with a kiss, her lips soft and insistent against Elena's. Elena melted into the embrace, her body molding to Mira's as if no time had passed at all.

This is where I belong, she thought, as Mira's hands slid down her back, pulling her closer. *This is where I've always belonged.*

And as they lost themselves in each other, the rest of the world falling away until there was nothing but the two of them, Elena knew that whatever challenges lay ahead, whatever obstacles they would have to face, they would face them together.

Because in the end, their love was stronger than anything that could come between them. And that was all that mattered.

* * *

The first rays of morning light filtered through the dusty windows of Harmony Hall, casting a soft glow over Elena and Mira as they sat side by side, their hands intertwined. The air around them felt charged with the weight of their shared history, the revelations of the night before still echoing in the silence.

Elena's heart raced as she turned to face Mira, her eyes searching the other woman's face for any sign of regret or uncertainty. But all she found was a mirror of her own emotions: a mix of fear, longing, and a desperate hope for a future they had once thought impossible.

"What do we do now?" Elena asked, her voice barely above a whisper. "After everything that's happened, how can we just...start over?"

Mira's grip on her hand tightened, a reassuring squeeze that sent a shiver down Elena's spine. "We take it one day at a time," she said softly, her green eyes shimmering with unshed tears. "We learn to trust each other again, to forgive each other for the mistakes we've made."

Elena nodded, her throat tight with emotion. She knew it wouldn't be easy, that there were still so many wounds to heal and barriers to overcome. But as she looked at Mira, at the woman she had loved for so long, she knew that it would be worth it.

We've wasted so much time already, she thought, her heart aching with the weight of their lost years. *I won't let my fears hold me back anymore.*

Slowly, tentatively, she reached out to brush a strand of hair from Mira's face, her fingers lingering on the soft skin of her cheek. Mira leaned into the touch, her eyes fluttering closed as a small sigh escaped her lips.

"I'm scared," Elena admitted, her voice trembling slightly. "I'm scared of getting hurt again, of losing you."

Mira's eyes opened, her gaze locking with Elena's. "I know," she said softly. "I'm scared too. But I'm also tired of running from my feelings, of pretending that I don't still love you."

Elena's breath caught in her throat at the words, her heart swelling with a hope she had never dared to allow herself to feel. "You...you still love me?" she whispered, her voice barely audible over the pounding of her own heart.

Mira nodded, a small smile tugging at the corners of her mouth. "I never stopped," she said simply. "Even when I hated you, even when I tried to convince myself that I was better off without you...I never stopped loving you."

Elena felt a tear slip down her cheek, the dam inside her finally breaking as years of pent-up emotion came rushing to the surface. She leaned forward, resting her forehead against Mira's as they both let the tears fall freely.

This is it, she thought, as Mira's arms wrapped around her, holding her close. *This is our second chance.*

And as the morning light grew brighter around them, chasing away the shadows of the past, Elena knew that whatever challenges lay ahead, they would face them together. Because in the end, their love was the only thing that mattered.

Eleven

ELENA SAVORED the warmth of Mira's embrace, the familiar scent of her perfume enveloping her in a cocoon of comfort and longing. The years of hurt and misunderstandings seemed to melt away, replaced by a sense of belonging that had been missing from her life for far too long.

As they pulled back, Mira's eyes sparkled with a renewed sense of hope, a tentative smile gracing her lips. "I know we can't erase the past," she said softly, her fingers gently brushing a stray lock of hair from Elena's face. "But maybe we can start over, build something new together."

Elena nodded, her heart swelling with a mixture of excitement and trepidation. "I want that more than anything," she whispered, her voice thick with emotion. "But I'm afraid of messing things up again, of losing you."

Mira's hand found Elena's, their fingers intertwining in a gesture of reassurance. "We're both different people now," she said, her gaze steady and unwavering. "We've grown, learned from our mistakes. I believe in us, Elena. I believe in the love we share."

Elena felt a surge of love and gratitude wash over her, the intensity of it nearly taking her breath away. She leaned in, her lips brushing against Mira's in a tender, lingering kiss. It was a promise, a vow to cherish and protect the precious bond they had rediscovered.

They found themselves slipping deeper into a world of desire as their hands, starting with a touch, explored each other's bodies. Thoughts clouded by the sensations overtaking them.

"You're so beautiful," Mira whispered against Elena's skin, trailing kisses down her neck and collarbone. Her hands roamed freely, tracing every curve and dip of Elena's body with possessive familiarity.

Elena shivered under Mira's touch, arching her back in silent invitation. "Do whatever you want with me," she breathed, her words tinged with arousal. "I'm yours."

Mira's eyes flashed as she pulled back to look at Elena, taking in her flushed cheeks and parted lips.

They moaned together, feeling hands stroking, moving in a slow, steady rhythm. Each touch sent shockwaves of pleasure coursing through their bodies, leaving them breathless and eager for more.

"That's it," Mira growled, her grip on Elena tightening. "Feel every inch of me."

Elena whimpered softly as she wrapped her arms around Mira, digging her nails into her shoulders in a show of submission and need. She could feel herself growing wetter, the sensation amplified by the anticipation building inside her.

"You like that?" Mira asked. A muffled moan escaped Elena's lips as she nodded fervently, unable to speak past the surge of pleasure coursing through every nerve ending in her body.

With renewed fierceness, Mira took control of their love-making, guiding them through a series of positions that left Elena panting and begging for mercy while simultaneously driving her wild with desire. Mira teased and tormented Elena's senses until she was certain she would scream from the intensity of it all.

And then finally—as if sensing that this was what she needed—she released control entirely, letting Elena take charge. Mira then eagerly obeyed Elena's silent commands —grateful for this unexpected gift of trust and freedom within their dynamic.

As they neared their climax together (or perhaps because they were so close), something snapped within both of them: an almost primal desire to claim ownership over each other physically manifested itself in their actions without warning or hesitation. Their love-making became rougher; their words harsher; their movements more possessive yet somehow also more tender than ever before...

Their bodies swaying gently to the rhythm of their synchronized heartbeats. The uncertainty of the future loomed before them, but in each other's arms, they found the strength and courage to face whatever lay ahead.

This is where we belong, Elena thought, her heart overflowing with a sense of peace and contentment. *Together, forever, no matter what challenges we may face.*

As they broke apart, the sounds of the world around them seemed to fade away, leaving only the two of them, lost in a moment of perfect understanding. Elena knew that the road ahead wouldn't be easy, that they would face challenges and obstacles, but with Mira by her side, she felt strong enough to take on anything.

This is our new beginning, she thought, as they stood hand in hand, ready to face the future together. *And this time, we'll make it right.*

The air between them hummed with a newfound sense of possibility, the weight of their shared history slowly dissolving into the promise of a brighter future.

Elena's heart swelled with a mixture of love and gratitude as she gazed into Mira's eyes, seeing in them a reflection of her own hopes and dreams. "I never thought I'd have this chance again," she murmured, her voice barely above a whisper. "To be here with you, to feel this way."

Mira's hand reached up, gently cupping Elena's cheek, her thumb tracing a delicate path along the soft skin. "I never stopped loving you," she confessed, her words carrying the weight of years of unspoken longing. "Even when I tried to convince myself otherwise, my heart always belonged to you."

Elena leaned into Mira's touch, savoring the warmth and comfort it provided. She closed her eyes, allowing herself to be swept away by the overwhelming surge of emotions that coursed through her veins. In that moment, the world around them ceased to exist, and all that mattered was the love they shared.

Elena and Mira sealed their love with a passionate, soul-searing kiss, their hearts entwined in an unbreakable bond that would endure through all of life's trials and triumphs.

Twelve

THE JOYOUS LAUGHTER of children filled the air, mingling with the chatter of eager parents as the Willow Creek Community Festival burst to life. Streamers swayed in the gentle breeze, and the aroma of fresh popcorn and cotton candy wafted through the crowd. Amidst the sea of faces, Elena Martinez stood with a guarded expression, her dark eyes scanning the surroundings.

Beside her, Mira Thompson fidgeted with the hem of her sundress, uncertainty flickering in her green eyes as she watched her daughter Chloe dart towards the children's activity area. The weight of their shared history hung between them, unspoken yet palpable.

"She seems excited," Elena remarked, her voice carefully neutral.

Mira nodded, a tentative smile playing on her lips. "She's been talking about this for weeks. I just hope..." Her words trailed off, swallowed by the noise of the festival.

Elena's gaze lingered on Mira for a moment, a flicker of understanding passing between them. They both knew the risks of letting their guard down, even for a moment.

As Chloe joined the throng of children around the face-painting booth, Elena and Mira found themselves drawn into the festive atmosphere. They watched as Chloe giggled with delight, her cheeks adorned with colorful butterflies and stars.

But in an instant, the carefree moment shattered.

Elena's heart lurched as she realized Chloe was no longer in sight. A sickening dread coiled in her stomach, and she grabbed Mira's arm instinctively. "Where's Chloe?"

Mira's face drained of color. "She was just there! I only looked away for a second..."

They surged forward, voices rising above the din as they called out Chloe's name. Elena's pulse pounded in her ears, a familiar fear clawing at her chest. She couldn't lose someone else, not like this.

Frantic, they wove through the crowd, eyes desperately searching for a glimpse of Chloe's blonde hair or the butterfly painted on her cheek. Each passing second felt like an eternity, the weight of their shared past bearing down on them.

"Chloe!" Mira's voice broke, raw with desperation.

Elena's mind raced through worst-case scenarios. She pushed them aside, focusing on the task at hand. They had to find Chloe. Nothing else mattered.

A flicker of movement caught Elena's eye. A small figure darted between booths, blonde hair gleaming in the sunlight. "There!" she shouted, pointing toward the edge of the festival grounds.

Mira's gaze followed, her face a mask of determination. Without a word, they broke into a run, feet pounding against the grass as they chased after Chloe's receding form. The world narrowed to a single point, the need to reach Chloe consuming their every thought.

As Elena raced toward the embankment leading down to the river, her heart hammered against her ribcage. The water rushed by, swollen from recent rains, its currents swift and unforgiving. "Chloe, stop!" Elena cried out, straining to be heard above the crowd.

But Chloe, lost in her own world of adventure, continued to scamper closer to danger.

Elena pushed herself harder, muscles burning as she closed the distance. Just as Chloe reached the edge, her foot slipped on the damp grass. Elena's heart stopped as she watched the little girl tumble forward.

With a final burst of speed, Elena lunged, arms outstretched. She caught Chloe around the waist, pulling her back just as the earth crumbled beneath them. They landed in a tangled heap on the grass, Chloe cradled protectively against Elena's chest.

"I've got you, sweetie," Elena whispered, her voice trembling with relief. "You're safe now."

Mira dropped to her knees beside them, tears streaming down her face as she gathered Chloe into her arms. "Don't ever scare us like that again," she murmured, pressing kisses to her daughter's hair.

As they held Chloe close, their bodies shaking from the aftermath of fear and adrenaline, Elena and Mira's eyes met over the top of the little girl's head. In that moment, years of hurt and resentment melted away, replaced by profound gratitude for the precious life they had almost lost.

"Mommy, I'm sorry," Chloe whispered, her small arms tightening around Mira's neck. "I didn't mean to wander off."

"It's okay, baby," Mira murmured, kissing her forehead. "You're safe now. That's all that matters."

Elena's heart swelled as she watched Mira hold Chloe close. Their eyes met, and for a moment, they were no longer rivals but two women bound by love for the child in their arms.

"I thought we'd lost her," Elena whispered, her voice raw.

Mira nodded, unable to speak past the lump in her throat. She reached out, her hand finding Elena's, their fingers intertwining in a silent promise.

    In that moment, Mira knew everything had changed. The unexpected crisis had stripped away layers of hurt, revealing the truth of what they meant to each other.

    "Let's find somewhere quiet," Elena suggested, her voice barely above a whisper.

    Mira nodded, cradling Chloe as they navigated the bustling crowd. They found a secluded bench beneath a sprawling oak tree, the distant sounds of the festival fading into the background.

    For a moment, they sat in silence, the weight of the situation hanging heavily between them. Elena's hand rested on Mira's, a lifeline in the tumultuous sea of emotions.

    "I can't believe we almost lost her," Mira murmured.

    Elena interjected, brushing her thumb over Mira's knuckles. "Chloe's safe now, thanks to you."

    Mira shook her head, a bitter laugh escaping her lips. "What kind of mother am I, letting her wander off like that?"

    Elena tightened her grip, her gaze fierce. "Don't do that to yourself. You're an incredible mother. This wasn't your fault."

    Mira's eyes glistened with unshed tears. "I can't help but think about what could have happened."

    "But we found her," Elena said firmly. "That's all that matters now."

Mira nodded, drawing in a shaky breath. She glanced at Chloe, who had drifted off to sleep, exhausted. The sight of her daughter's peaceful face filled Mira with profound relief.

"I don't know what I would have done if you hadn't been here," Mira admitted, meeting Elena's gaze. "I couldn't have faced this alone."

Elena's expression softened. "You're not alone, Mira. Not anymore. When it comes to Chloe, we're in this together."

A surge of gratitude washed over Mira. For so long, she had carried the burden of her mistakes, convinced she had to face the world alone. But now, with Elena by her side, she dared to hope that perhaps she didn't have to be alone anymore.

As they sat together beneath the oak tree, Mira felt a sense of peace wash over her. The unexpected event had shaken them but also brought them closer, reminding them of the bond they shared.

"Elena," Mira whispered, her voice trembling. "I know we have a lot to work through, but I want you to know that I'm here. I'm ready to face whatever comes our way, together."

Elena's breath caught. She reached out, intertwining their fingers. The simple gesture conveyed the unspoken promise of a shared future.

Chloe lifted her head, looking between them with

curiosity. "Mommy, Elena, can we stay like this for a little longer?"

Mira smiled softly, kissing Chloe's forehead. "Of course, sweetheart. We have all the time in the world."

As the sun began to dip below the horizon, casting a golden glow, Elena and Mira shared a knowing look. The path ahead would be filled with challenges, but they knew they had the strength to face them together. With Chloe as their guiding light, they would navigate the uncharted waters of their relationship, determined to build a future filled with healing and endless possibilities.

As the laughter of the community event faded, they made their way to the parking lot. The cool evening breeze carried the scent of blooming flowers, soothing their frayed nerves. The sky was painted in hues of orange and pink, the setting sun casting long shadows.

With each step, the tension began to dissipate, replaced by a newfound sense of unity. Elena's hand remained intertwined with Mira's, their fingers fitting together like missing pieces. Chloe skipped alongside them, her innocent laughter a reminder of the bond they shared.

Approaching Elena's car, Mira paused, turning to face her. "Elena, I..." she began, her voice trembling. "I don't know how to thank you for today."

Elena's gaze softened. "You don't have to thank me. I will always be here for you and Chloe."

Mira's eyes glistened with unshed tears. She drew Elena into a tight embrace, burying her face in the crook of her neck. Elena inhaled the familiar scent of lavender and vanilla.

Chloe, not wanting to be left out, wiggled between them, her small arms encircling their legs. "I love you, Mommy. I love you, Elena," she declared, her voice filled with pure love.

Elena and Mira exchanged a glance, their hearts swelling for the little girl who had brought them back together. They knelt, enveloping Chloe in a group hug, their laughter mingling with the gentle rustle of leaves.

As they stood up, Elena's hand found Mira's once more, their fingers interlacing with a sense of belonging. "Let's go home," she whispered, carrying the promise of a future yet to be written.

Mira nodded, a soft smile gracing her features. She helped Chloe into the car before sliding into the passenger side. Elena took her place behind the wheel, the engine roaring to life.

As they drove away from the community event, the sun dipped below the horizon, painting the sky with stars. The road stretched out before them, a metaphor for the journey ahead. They knew the path would be filled with twists and turns, but they were determined to face each challenge together, their love guiding them every step.

In the rearview mirror, Elena caught a glimpse of

Chloe's sleeping form, her head lolling to the side. A warm smile tugged at Elena's lips, her heart swelling with the realization that this precious child had become an integral part of her life.

Mira reached over, her hand finding Elena's thigh and giving it a gentle squeeze. The gesture conveyed the depth of her gratitude and the promise of a future intertwined.

As the car disappeared into the night, the lingering scent of lavender and vanilla drifted through the air, a reminder of rekindled love and forged bonds. Elena and Mira knew that the road ahead would be filled with challenges, but they were ready to face them head-on, their hearts beating as one, their love a beacon guiding them through the darkness.

* * *

As the car wound its way through the quiet streets of Willow Creek, Elena found herself lost in thought, replaying the day's events like a vivid dream. The fear that had gripped her heart when Chloe disappeared, the overwhelming relief that flooded through her veins when they found her safe, and the inexplicable connection that had sparked between her and Mira during those moments of shared vulnerability.

She glanced over at Mira, her profile illuminated by the soft glow of the streetlights. The years had changed them both, but in that moment, Elena saw a flicker of the girl she had once known—the girl who had captured her heart with infectious laughter and boundless spirit.

"I never thought I'd be here again," Elena murmured, her voice barely audible over the hum of the engine. "With you, I mean."

Mira turned to face her, green eyes shimmering with a mix of emotions. "Life has a funny way of bringing us back to where we're meant to be," she said softly, intertwining her fingers with Elena's.

The touch sent a shiver down Elena's spine, igniting a spark that had lain dormant for far too long. She inhaled deeply, the scent of Mira's perfume mingling with the faint aroma of Chloe's strawberry shampoo, creating a heady cocktail that made her head spin.

In that moment, Elena realized that the unexpected event at the community gathering had been a catalyst, a turning point in their story. It had stripped away the layers of hurt and anger that had built up over the years, revealing the raw, vulnerable truth beneath.

As they pulled up to Mira's house, anticipation thrummed through Elena's veins. She knew the road ahead would be far from easy, that they would have to navigate the complexities of their past and the challenges of their present. But for the first time in years, she felt a glimmer of hope, a whisper of possibility that made her heart race.

Mira turned off the engine, the sudden silence enveloping them like a cocoon. She faced Elena, eyes searching, lips parted as if on the verge of speech. Instead of words, she leaned in, her breath ghosting over Elena's skin as she pressed a soft, lingering kiss to her cheek.

"Thank you," she whispered, her voice thick with emotion. "For being there today, for being here now."

Elena swallowed hard, her throat tight with the weight of unspoken words. She reached up, cupping Mira's face in her hands, her thumb tracing the delicate curve of her cheekbone. "I'll always be here," she murmured, the promise hanging in the air between them like a sacred vow.

As they sat in the darkness, the rest of the world fell away. Elena knew this was just the beginning. The unexpected event had set them on a new path, a journey of rediscovery and reconnection that would test their strength and resolve. But with Mira by her side and Chloe's love to guide them, she felt that anything was possible.

In that moment, as their hearts beat in unison, Elena understood that they were no longer defined by their past. They were on the brink of something new—a shared future filled with healing, laughter, and love.

Thirteen

THE DIM GLOW of the Edison bulbs hanging from the exposed rafters cast a seductive sheen over the polished mahogany bar of The Ember Lounge. A lone saxophonist crooned a sultry melody that wove through the murmur of conversation and clink of glasses. Elena Martinez stood behind the bar, hair cascading down her back like spilled ink, the dark waves a stark contrast to the crisp white of her button-down shirt. Her fingers absently traced the edges of a coaster as her eyes scanned the room, searching, always searching, for a glimpse of blonde hair and green eyes that still haunted her dreams.

And then, there she was again. Mira Thompson stepped out of the shadows of a secluded booth in the far corner, the sight of her hitting Elena like a physical blow. The years had been kind to Mira - the planes of her face more defined, the softness of youth sharpened into the sculptured elegance of a woman who had weathered storms and emerged stronger. But her eyes, those moss green eyes that Elena had once been able to read like a favorite novel, remained shuttered and unreadable.

Elena's heart pounded a staccato beat against her ribcage as she stepped out from behind the bar, her movements fluid and purposeful despite the tremor in her hands. She wove through the tables, the hem of her black slacks brushing against the hardwood with each step, until she stood before Mira, close enough to catch the subtle notes of her perfume - jasmine and regret.

Mira's voice trembled as she finally spoke, each word a fragile offering in the face of Elena's anger. "I never meant to hurt you, Elena. I know my actions caused you pain, and I've carried that regret with me every day since."

Her eyes glistened with tears, the green depths swirling with a tempest of emotions - remorse, longing, and a desperate plea for understanding. "There were reasons, things I couldn't tell you then. Mistakes I made, choices that haunt me still. But please, believe me when I say that leaving you was the hardest thing I've ever had to do."

Elena's heart clenched at the raw vulnerability in Mira's voice, the walls she had so carefully constructed around her heart beginning to crack under the weight of Mira's words. She wanted to cling to her anger, to the familiar armor of resentment that had shielded her for so long. But as she looked into Mira's eyes, she saw a reflection of her own pain, a shared history of love and loss that bound them together, even now.

"Then why?" Elena whispered, her voice barely audible above the pounding of her heart. "Why did you leave, Mira? Why didn't you trust me enough to let me in, to let me help you face whatever it was that drove you away?"

Mira's hand twitched at her side, as if aching to reach out and bridge the distance between them. "I was scared, Elena. Scared of my own mistakes, scared of dragging you down with me. I thought I was protecting you by leaving, but I see now that I was only running from my own demons."

A single tear escaped down Mira's cheek, glistening in the muted light of the lounge. "I never stopped loving you, Elena. Even when I couldn't be with you, even when I thought I didn't deserve your love, it was always there, burning inside me like an unquenchable flame."

Elena's breath caught in her throat, the anger that had fueled her for so long beginning to dissipate in the face of Mira's honesty. She could see the truth in Mira's eyes.

Mira reached out a trembling hand, her fingers brushing against Elena's cheek in a tender gesture of longing and regret. The touch was feather-light, a whisper of skin against skin, yet it sent a shiver down Elena's spine. Time seemed to stand still as Mira's fingertips traced the contours of Elena's face, mapping out the familiar terrain of a love that had never truly faded.

Elena's breath hitched in her throat, her body betraying her as she leaned into Mira's touch. It was a gesture so achingly familiar, a reminder of countless moments stolen in the shadows of their past. Elena's eyes fluttered closed for a brief moment, savoring the warmth of Mira's skin against her own.

When she opened her eyes again, all Elena saw was a reflection of her own longing, a mirror of the love that had never died, despite the wounds they had inflicted upon each other.

Mira's voice was barely above a whisper as she spoke, her words a plea for forgiveness. "I'm so sorry, Elena. For everything. I know I hurt you, and I can't take that back. But I'm here now, and I'm not going anywhere. Not unless you tell me to."

Mira's hand slid from Elena's cheek to the back of her neck, her fingers tangling in the silky strands of dark hair. "I'm scared too, Elena. Scared of losing you, of never being able to make things right between us. But I'm even more scared of living a life without you in it."

Elena's heart raced in her chest, each beat a reminder of the love that still pulsed beneath the surface of her skin.

"I never stopped loving you, Mira," she whispered, the words feeling like a weight lifted from her soul. "Even when I tried to hate you, even when I convinced myself that I was better off without you, my heart never let go."

Mira's eyes glistened with unshed tears, her lips curving into a smile that was equal parts joy and relief. "I never stopped loving you either, Elena. You were always the one, the only one who ever truly understood me."

Elena's hand found Mira's, their fingers intertwining in a silent promise of forgiveness and hope. The warmth of Mira's skin against her own felt like coming home, like finding a piece of herself that had been missing for far too long.

In that moment, the past seemed to fall away, the hurt and the anger and the betrayal fading into the background of their story. All that mattered was the present, the feel of Mira's body pressed against her own, the promise of a future that they could build together.

And as their lips met in a kiss that was both tender and passionate, Elena knew that she was exactly where she was meant to be. In the arms of the woman she loved, ready to face whatever challenges lay ahead, as long as they faced them together.

Mira's voice trembled as she spoke, her words a fragile echo in the dimly lit corner of The Ember Lounge. "Elena, I know I've hurt you in ways I can never fully atone for, but..." She paused, her breath catching in her throat as she searched Elena's face for a glimmer of hope. "Is there a chance for us? To rebuild what we once had, to find solace in each other's arms once again?"

Elena's heart raced, the weight of Mira's question hanging heavy in the air between them. The scent of Mira's perfume, a delicate blend of jasmine and sandalwood, enveloped her senses, stirring memories of stolen moments and whispered promises from a lifetime ago.

As she gazed into Mira's eyes, Elena saw the depths of her own longing reflected back at her. The years of pain and anger that had built a fortress around her heart began to crumble, brick by brick, as the realization of Mira's sincerity washed over her.

With a shaky hand, Elena reached out, her fingertips grazing the soft skin of Mira's cheek. A single tear escaped her eye, tracing a glistening path down her face as she whispered, "I've never stopped wanting that, Mira. Even when I tried to convince myself otherwise."

Mira leaned into Elena's touch, her eyes fluttering closed as a wave of relief and gratitude surged through her. "I know I have a lot to prove, but I'm willing to do whatever it takes to earn your trust again, to show you that my love for you has never wavered."

Elena's hand slid down Mira's arm, her fingers intertwining with Mira's in a silent promise of forgiveness and a second chance. The warmth of their joined hands seemed to radiate through her entire being, chasing away the chill of the past and igniting a spark of hope for the future.

As they stood there, hands clasped and hearts beating in sync, the world around them faded away. The soft murmur of conversations and the clinking of glasses became distant echoes, mere background noise to the profound connection that had always existed between them.

Mira's lips quivered as she leaned in, the warmth of her breath mingling with Elena's in the scant space between them. With a tender intensity, Mira closed the remaining distance, her lips brushing against Elena's in a kiss that was both gentle and passionate. The contact ignited a fire within her, a blaze that had been smoldering beneath the ashes of their past. Elena's lips, soft and inviting, moved against Mira's with a familiar rhythm, a dance they had once known by heart.

As the kissed deepened, Mira's hands found their way to Elena's waist, pulling her closer until their bodies were flush against each other. The heat of Elena's skin seeped through the fabric of her dress, igniting a trail of goosebumps along Mira's arms. Every nerve ending in Mira's body came alive, electrified by the sensation of Elena's touch, the taste of her lips, and the scent of her perfume—a heady combination that threatened to overwhelm her senses.

Mira poured every ounce of her love, her longing, and

her remorse into the kiss, silently communicating the depths of her feelings for Elena. The years of separation melted away, and for a fleeting moment, it felt as though they had never been apart, as if their hearts had always been intertwined, waiting for this moment of reunion.

Elena pulled back slightly, her breath coming in shallow gasps as she searched Mira's face for confirmation. Her eyes, dark and introspective, held a silent question—a plea for reassurance that they could truly move forward together, leaving the pain of the past behind. Mira met Elena's gaze, her own eyes shimmering with a mix of hope and uncertainty.

Can we really do this? Elena's eyes seemed to ask, vulnerability etched into every line of her face. *Can we rebuild what we once had, or will the ghosts of our past always haunt us?*

In that moment, with Elena in her arms and the taste of her lips still lingering on her tongue, Mira knew that she was willing to face anything to be with the woman she loved.

Mira's eyes shone with newfound determination as she held Elena's gaze, her voice filled with quiet conviction. "We can do this, Elena. Together." Her words a promise and a vow. "I know the road ahead won't be easy, but I'm willing to face whatever challenges come our way, as long as I have you by my side."

Elena's heart swelled with a mix of relief and joy at Mira's declaration.

Mira reached out and gently cupped Elana's face, her thumb brushing away a stray tear that had escaped from the corner of Elena's eye. The touch was tender, almost reverent, and it sent a shiver down Elena's spine. "I know I hurt you in the past, Elena," Mira whispered, her voice thick with emotion. "And I know that it will take time for you to trust me again. But I promise you, I will spend every day proving to you that my love for you is true, that I will never leave your side again."

Elena leaned into Mira's touch, her eyes fluttering closed for a brief moment as she savored the warmth of her skin against her own. She surged forward, capturing Mira's lips in a searing kiss that spoke of forgiveness, of second chances, and of a love that had never truly died. And as they held each other close, their hearts beating in unison.

Their embrace tightened as the world around them faded into a distant hum, the warmth of their bodies melding together in a symphony of reconciliation. Elena's fingers traced the delicate curve of Mira's spine, each touch a silent promise to cherish and protect the love they had fought so hard to reclaim. Mira's hands, in turn, tangled in Elena's dark tresses, anchoring herself to the reality of this moment, to the woman she had once feared lost forever.

As they pulled back, just enough to gaze into each other's eyes, Elena saw a glimmer of the future reflected in Mira's tear-stained face. A future where the scars of their past would fade, where trust would be rebuilt brick by brick, and where their love would grow stronger with each passing day. She knew it wouldn't be easy, that there would be moments of doubt and fear, but in the steadfast determination of Mira's gaze, she found the courage to believe.

"We're going to make it," Elena whispered, her voice filled with a quiet conviction. "You and me, together. No matter what."

Mira nodded, a watery smile tugging at the corners of her lips. "No matter what," she echoed, sealing the promise with another gentle press of her lips against Elena's.

And as they stood there, wrapped in each other's arms, the soft glow of the Ember Lounge casting a warm halo around their entwined silhouettes, Elena and Mira knew that they had finally found their way home. Home to each other, to the love they had once thought lost, and to the hope of a future that shimmered with the promise of forever.